MW01603057

DECLUTTERED AND DEAD

A LILY SPRAYBERRY REALTOR COZY MYSTERY

CAROLYN RIDDER ASPENSON

Severn River
PUBLISHING

DECLUTTERED AND DEAD

Severn River Publishing
www.SevernRiverPublishing.com

ISBN: 978-1-64875-904-8 (Paperback)

ACKNOWLEDGMENTS

Thank you to my wonderful editor, Jen, my favorite proofreader, JC Wing, my favorite beta reader, Lynn Shaw, and my friends and family who've supported me as I've traveled along this writing journey.

ABOUT CAROLYN

Carolyn Ridder Aspenson writes sassy, southern cozy mysteries featuring imperfect women with a flair for telling it like it is. Her stories focus on relationships, whether they're between friends, family members, couples, townspeople, or strangers, because ultimately, it's relationships that make a story.

Now an empty-nester, Carolyn lives in the Atlanta suburbs with her husband, two Pit Bull-Boxer mix dogs and two cantankerous cats, but you'll often find her at a local coffee shop people-watching (and listening.) Or as she likes to call it: plotting her next novel.

Join Carolyn's mailing list at
CarolynRidderAspenson.com

CPSIA information can be obtained
at www.ICGtesting.com
Printed in the USA
BVHW032151010421
603992BV00015B/122

9 781648 759048

ALSO BY CAROLYN RIDDER ASPENSON

The Lily Sprayberry Realtor Cozy Mystery Series

Deal Gone Dead

Decluttered and Dead

Signed, Sealed and Dead

Bidding War Break-In

Open House Heist

Realtor Rub Out

Foreclosure Fatality

Lily Sprayberry Novellas

The Scarecrow Snuff Out

The Claus Killing

Santa's Little Thief

The Chantilly Adair Paranormal Cozy Mystery Series

Get Up and Ghost

Ghosts Are People Too

Praying For Peace

Ghost From the Grave

Haunting Hooligans: A Chantilly Adair Novella

The Pooch Party Cozy Mystery Series

Pooches, Pumpkins, and Poison

Hounds, Harvest, and Homicide

Dogs, Dinners, and Death

Join Carolyn's Newsletter List at

CarolynRidderAspenson.com

You'll receive a free novella as a thank you!

For Mary Ann Ridder
Thank you for encouraging my love for mysteries.

To be notified of future releases and receive a free book, visit
CarolynRidderAspenson.com

CHAPTER 1

*S*ecrets are never really secret, especially in a small town.

"**B**o, heel." I stood ramrod straight with the vibration controller in hand, ready to press the button on my Boxer mix puppy's collar if he didn't heel to my side. His crazy-legged gallop, the one where his big feet flopped all over the place from pure uncontrollable excitement, screeched to a halt, and he backed up, placing himself into the heeled position by my right side.

I beamed with pride. Bo was only four months old, but he'd already grown out of his puppy stage and into a clumsy forty-pound lump of drooling, rock-like muscle lap dog. The muscle that left a multi-colored bruise when it plowed into the side of my leg. I'd started the two of us in training, and so far, we'd done well. Actually, Bo did better than me. I was a softy, and I needed to toughen up so he didn't get mixed signals. It wasn't easy though, with those big puppy eyes staring at me as they did.

We stayed in heel position until we walked closer to the dog park entrance inside Castleberry Park. Bo's tail wagged blissfully, and he stuck his little booty in the air with his front paws down, in what I called his puppy play mode, when he saw all of his friends rush to the fence to bark their hellos. "Bo, sit."

He sat.

I completely understood how parents felt when their kids did something wonderful. Sure, Bo wasn't a human kid, but he was my baby, and for me, the fact that he had four legs and a tail didn't matter. His daily accomplishments were also mine, and they made me happy. I removed the leash and said okay, and he rushed off to the fence gate. Another dog owner opened it, greeted Bo with a cheerful hello and pat on the head, which he acknowledged with a tail wag and then bolted off to play.

After thirty minutes of tumbling and rough-housing with the other dogs, I had to drag him out practically kicking and screaming like a toddler. We needed to practice our off-leash training on the park's path before meeting the not-yet-labeled man in my life, Dylan Roberts.

Castleberry Park was the largest of three Bramblett County recreational parks. The county built it two years ago to accommodate the increased popularity of lacrosse, and teams from all over the state flocked to tournaments there every season except winter because it was the only one in northern Georgia with eleven turf lacrosse fields. With the pressure of local dog owners, the county added the dog park to an unused, lightly wooded area about nine months ago. The paved multi-use path outlining the park was perfect for practicing off leash training with Bo. Though technically the law stated all dogs must be on a leash no longer than six feet, it was early enough that the morning walkers didn't complain, and since the not-yet-defined man in my life just happened to be the county Sheriff, I flat out broke that law. I figured I'd get off with a warning, at least the first time I got caught.

In my defense, I wasn't the only one that did it, though my

momma would tell me that's no excuse and question if I'd jump off a bridge because everyone did it, but technically speaking, the electronic collar was a leash, and I had more control over Bo with the controller than I did with an actual physical strap, so I would argue that point in court any day if I had to. I just hoped it never came to that.

We'd spent twenty minutes walking part of the two-mile path and made it to the section connecting to the exit path that connected to Gibson Bridge. Nose to the ground, Bo followed a scent to the right and onto that path. The bridge was about a half mile up, and it was his most favorite place on earth. An ideal spot for local photographers and artists, the old covered wood walking bridge didn't actually lead anywhere anymore unless one wanted to cross the rocky stream to fish or swim. Bo liked to watch the fish jump out of the water. They fascinated him. He'd try to catch them with his drooling mouth and droopy jowls but wasn't quick enough.

The covered section of the bridge was my favorite place to hang out, mostly because of the shade. It leaned just a bit to the left, and years of teenagers carving their true loves names into the old wood was considered damage by some, but I thought of it as a touch of history and nostalgia. Yes, Dylan and I had our names carved into it, too, which was why I thought of the carvings as nostalgic rather than damaging. Our long-term high school and college relationship had been intense and hadn't ended well, but he wanted to give it another try, and considering I was still in love with him, I couldn't deny the chance. I just had to take it slow because I didn't trust that he wouldn't up and leave me again.

"You feel like going that way, big guy?" I checked my watch. We still had a good fifteen minutes before we had to meet Dylan, so I figured why not?

I sent Dylan a quick text telling him we'd veered off toward the bridge and might be a few minutes late just in case.

"The nose goes where the nose goes," he replied.

Up ahead I caught a glimpse of my high school friend and college sorority sister, Heather Barrington walking with a man with short brown hair and a scruffy beard I thought looked like William Abernathy. William's family owned the biggest and most popular corn maze and pumpkin patch in the surrounding area. Another high school and college friend, Caroline Abernathy, married William shortly after college. As I walked Bo toward them, the man turned off the path and cut through the wooded section.

Heather and Caroline were best friends then, and best friends still, and both were signed up to be in my Decluttering and Staging Your Home for Sale class starting later that morning.

Bo greeted Heather with a nose bump to a somewhat private place. He had no shame, but it embarrassed me. "Bo, heel."

He backed up and stood by my side.

"Sorry about that. We're still learning our manners."

She waved it off. "Oh, honey, he's a dog. That's how they say hey." She bent down and patted Bo's head. "I'm looking forward to class today. Should be a lot of fun. Will Belle be there?"

Belle Pyott, my best friend and business partner, also went to school with Heather and me.

"She'll come by, but she's not staying for the entire class."

She blew out a breath and puffed her bottom lip out into a pout. "That's too bad. Funny, we all live in the same town and rarely see each other."

"Caroline will be there, too, but you probably already knew that. Hey, was that William I just saw with you?"

She twirled a strand of her long red hair around her finger. "William? Oh, heavens, no. That was a client. He's looking for a painting of the bridge. Wanted to see if I was interested in doing one for him."

I nodded even though it sure looked like William to me.

We caught up as we walked toward the main path. "Well, I have to meet someone, but I'll see you an hour or so," I said.

She smiled. "Yes, I hear you're back together with Dylan. You sure latched onto that tall drink of water right quick when he got back to town."

And that's when I remembered why we'd stopped hanging out. My momma once said there were two types of women, One type a man brings home to his momma, and the other type a man brings home, but not to the house his momma lived in. She also said girls went to college for one of two types of degrees, either a degree from the university itself or an M-R-S degree. She believed Heather Barrington went to college thinking she was the bring her home to momma kind of girl and wanted that M-R-S degree, but when she realized that wasn't in the cards, she'd flipped sides. Based on Heather's comment, I had to agree with my momma.

I didn't want her to make a play for Dylan, not that I thought he'd fall for it, but because we'd been friends since elementary school. That would be all kinds of awkward, her throwing herself into the mix of my sort of relationship with my one true love, but I also didn't feel right saying something that wasn't entirely true. "We're testing the waters." The truth was, yes, Dylan was back in town, and yes, we were spending time together, but the relationship itself hadn't yet been defined. I knew I loved him. I'd always loved him, but slow and steady won the race, and I was in no hurry to get to the finish line. Thankfully, Dylan understood.

"Well, that boy's got a mighty fine physique to go swimming with. He's all grown up now, that's for sure." She giggled, but it was more of an evil laugh than one filled with humor. "Keep an eye on that one. Someone might just sneak up behind you and steal him out from under you if you don't."

Gee, was that a threat of some sort? Had she let me know she'd planned to make a play for my man? Was he even really my man? Ugh. As if I needed that kind of additional stress in my life, especially given the fact that Heather would be in my face every day for the next week.

"Ta ta," she said, heading in the other direction. She turned around a second or two later. "Oh, Lily, I'd be tickled pink if you'd put one of my paintings up in your office. I'm into reds right now. They really add a pop of color." She wiggled her head and flicked her hair back. "I mean, look at my hair. Men just adore it, and you know what they say about us gingers. I bet one of my paintings would bring in all kinds of business."

Did she actually just threaten to take my man and then try to sell me her artwork? Wow. If I remembered correctly, the saying about gingers referred to them having no souls, though I doubted that's the one she meant.

Bless her heart. She wanted to sell her work so bad she'd resorted to comparing it to her floozy ways. I had half a mind to tell her that sales technique wouldn't work on women, but she might could give it a try on some of the older men in town. I would have bet good money on Old Man Goodson buying her self-portrait and hanging it right next to the 50s girl pin up calendar in his shop.

If my momma knew what I was thinking she'd have sent me outside to pick the thinnest switch on a tree in my backyard and then whacked me on the back of the thighs with it. I was ashamed of myself for my nasty thoughts, especially because they were about an old friend.

I didn't want one of Heather's paintings, but I almost pitied her because I knew her life hadn't turned out the way she'd expected. Heather planned to marry rich and paint without worry of supporting herself. Instead, she still lived at home with her parents and worked at their store while trying to sell her paintings on the side. That had to crush the ego. "I'll talk to Belle, see what we can do." I smiled, knowing Belle thought a blind cow could paint better than our old friend. Belle didn't have an eye for art. It wasn't just Heather's. "See you in a bit."

She waved and skipped off. "Ta ta, love."

Bo and I met up with Dylan a few minutes later.

"Why the long face?" he asked.

I ignored the old joke reference that referred to the person resembling a horse because I knew he hadn't gone there. "I just ran into Heather Barrington."

"And?"

"I suggest you watch your back."

He glanced behind him. "Hard to do when it's behind me."

I rolled my eyes. "You know what I mean."

"Okay. Done. Care to tell me why though?"

"Because she'll probably leave claw marks in it if you don't."

"Noted." He brushed the back of his hand across my face. "Did you tell her I only have eyes for you?"

"I didn't think that would be appropriate."

"Then I promise, if she tries to get her claws into me, I'll make sure she knows."

I had a feeling the sheriff's office wouldn't have any Heather Barrington original artwork hanging in it any time soon.

"So, you know that secret client I've been working with for the past two weeks?"

He nodded. "The one that's taken you away from your favorite crime TV shows?"

"I have cable, you know. I can watch them on On Demand."

"That's too bad. You also have a real-life crime fighter right here." He pointed to his chest, which, I had to admit, was quite sexy in the tight-fitting t-shirt stuck to him from the sweat of his run.

"You're a small-town sheriff. The crime rate here is what, negative twenty?"

"It went up with the two murders you were involved in, remember?"

"I wasn't actually involved in them."

The corner of his mouth twitched, and I nearly melted right there. "So, go on."

"Okay, so this client is an old friend." I tapped the side of my leg, and Bo heeled to me. I wanted to do my happy dance, but per the trainer, I acted like it was no big deal. "And she's back in town to help sell her parent's house, so she's decided to go ahead and take my decluttering class even though we've finished the job on her parents place already."

"That's odd. Did you not do a good job on the place?"

I nudged him with my shoulder. "Of course I did. That's not why she's taking it. She was scheduled in it anyway, but I think she's taking it because of the other people registered. I'm pretty sure she wants to make a statement."

"Who is it?"

"Someone that's going to make my life miserable and cause a ton of conflict in the class just by showing up."

I could almost see his brain working. Dylan also grew up in Bramblett County, and he knew everyone I knew, so it took him less than a minute to figure it out.

He laughed. "You've got to be kidding me? Savannah Emmerson?"

I nodded. "Belle set this up. I think she does this stuff to me on purpose."

"Belle. Of course she does." He laughed harder. "That's hilarious. It's going to be a train wreck. I can't believe you're going through with it."

"What other option do I have?"

"You could tell her not to come."

"That wouldn't be very nice. Besides, she's offered to use her parent's house as an example for the class, and it looks great. Belle and I are even using it in our company portfolio. What am I supposed to do, say thanks for letting us use your folks home for our stuff, but hey, you're not welcome to the class because you're a floozy and pretty much everyone in the class hates you?"

"Maybe if you chose better words?"

I bowed my head and moaned. "This is going to be a disaster."

Savannah, Caroline, Heather, Belle, and I all hung out in the same social circle growing up, and in college, the five of us joined the same sorority at the University of Georgia. Things were great for a short time there, but Savannah ripped the group to shreds when she slept with Heather's boyfriend, Austin Emmerson, our sophomore year at UGA. Rumor had it she also slept with Caroline's boyfriend, now husband, but that was never confirmed. Savannah eventually married Austin and moved to Atlanta. In the process of a divorce, she came back to Bramblett County under the guise of helping her parents get their house organized and sold while they headed north to their retirement home in Maine. That's when she hired me and when Belle decided to sign her up for the decluttering class.

"Do you want me to send a deputy to make sure no fights break out?" The mouth twitch thing happened again.

"Don't joke. I might seriously need that."

We walked with Bo schlepping along in between us stopping every few seconds to smell or examine something interesting on the ground. "Makes sense now."

"What?"

"I ran into Austin Emmerson last night at Willy's."

"Really? Did he say anything?"

"About what?"

"The divorce."

"Sort of. He said something about a fight they'd had, how she'd screwed him out of a lot of money, but that's about it. I figured he was just blowing off steam."

"She hasn't really said much to me. You know how rumors spread around here, she probably wants to keep it on the downlow."

"Especially about her."

We made it back to the parking lot where he'd parked his black, four-door sheriff's car next to my car. "My poor car."

"What? Your car is great," he said.

"Next to your monstrosity it looks like one of those little Matchbox cars." I rubbed the roof. "I feel bad for it."

"I'm the sheriff. I need a big, manly car. Image is everything."

I laughed. "If that's true, then I'm a dainty little southern gal."

He kissed my forehead. "And that's what I love best about you."

I blushed. His expression was sincere, while I'd been kidding. I'd not really thought of myself as dainty, so it surprised me to think he did. "Thank you for taking Bo to doggy daycare today. I appreciate it." I hugged and kissed my puppy goodbye.

"Anything to win points with the mutt." He kissed my forehead again as Bo jumped into the back of his vehicle. "And you, of course."

I hadn't told him yet, but he'd already won back most of the points he'd lost years ago. "Okay, I'm off to get ready to referee this class. Stopping at the office and then getting some treats at Millie's first. Hopefully, that'll ease the shock when Savannah walks in."

"Good luck."

"Thanks, I'm going to need it." I blew him a kiss as he pulled away.

~

I'd pre-ordered a variety of baked goods and two jugs of sweet tea from Millie's, so they'd be ready for pick up when I stopped by. The county library where we'd decided to hold the decluttering class was just hop away from the bakery café, which was just another hop away from my office, but since I had all of the materials for the class along with the food and drinks, I still needed to drive. I loaded the yummy baked goods into my car and headed the block to the library.

The library was in desperate need of an update. I loved the smell and feel of old libraries. Their walls filled from floor to ceiling with shelves of books. I could wander the sectioned areas, run my fingertips across the spines of old hardcovers and paperbacks, breathe in the smell of the ink and paper.

The Bramblett County library lacked the character of an old library, the kind writers flocked to for research and readers went to just soak in the environment, to be one with the written word. It was just mechanical, necessary even, and felt old and dingy. The incandescent lighting gave the white walls a yellowish hue, though I suspected they were that way also because they needed a fresh coat of paint. The bookshelves weren't the dark, antique kind one might find in a big city library, but rather the kind from a retro 70s library, created by some art deco designer with an addiction to maple wood. And the place didn't smell like old books. It smelled like burnt coffee. Every time I walked in, I was immediately disappointed. I knew what awaited me inside, but nonetheless, I expected something different, and every time, I ended up disappointed.

The head librarian, Ellie Jean Pruitt, who'd also been my high school librarian, greeted me at the front desk. "Well, hey there, Miss Lilybit. I got the conference room all set up for you." She walked from behind the desk and picked up one of my bags. "Let me help you with that. Follow me, and I'll show you where you're going to be for the next few days."

"Thank you so much."

Ellie Jean had a daughter named Faith. She was my age, so Ellie Jean had to have been around my parent's age, but you wouldn't know it by looking at her. She fit the typical librarian stereotype. Old lady glasses with little points on the sides, her graying hair pulled into a tight bun and a floral print dress that fit her like a potato sack. It hit her larger than normal chest and hung down, without any shape, to her knees. She'd been married once, but her husband left town when their daughter was two and never returned. I couldn't help but think it was because of the potato sack dresses, but I kept that thought to myself.

Like my momma always said, "if you can't say something nice, shut your pie hole". Granted, she said that in the privacy of our home, and mostly to my brothers, but her words stuck with me, too.

"You're going to be in this room here." She opened the door to a plain but bright room, at least bright in comparison to the rest of the place. The back wall was actually the side of the building and lined with windows, allowing in nice natural light.

I glanced down at the chairs. The red cushions had faded from the sun. "If you keep the blinds closed when no one's using the room, the color on the cushions won't fade as quickly."

"Oh dear." She pulled out a chair and gasped. "They really are faded, aren't they? I'll have to talk to the board about replacing them."

Belle showed up a few minutes after I finished setting up the conference room. That wasn't unusual for her. I wasn't always prompt—one of my annoying bad habits—but Belle rarely arrived on time. I made a point of telling her events began thirty minutes early when I needed her there on time. The decluttering class set-up though, I could handle on my own. Besides, she organized the class, so I couldn't fudge the start time without her catching on.

She plopped into a chair and fanned herself, her long black hair pulled into a clip instead of styled to the hilt as usual. I eyed her up and down, and she caught on quickly. "Do not start with me. I barely slept a wink last night."

"If you're going to hoot with the owls, you'd better be able to soar with the eagles the next day."

"Honey, this gal did no hooting last night. I had a sinus headache the size of Killamon-whatever it's called. What in heaven's name is up with this weather anyway? My poor nose can't figure out if it should be clear or clogged."

"It's horrible, I'll give you that."

She rubbed her temples. "Stop talking so loud." She glanced at me with her blood shot eyes. "Do you have sinus medicine or anything I can take? My head is pounding."

I laughed. "You sure are a hot mess." I pointed to the other side of the room where I'd set my bag. "I think I've got something in there."

She dragged herself to my bag. "Hey, I forgot to tell you who I saw over at the old First Baptist Church yesterday."

"Who?"

"William Abernathy."

"Really? That's odd."

"What's even more odd is he was walking out of it with Heather Barrington."

"That's interesting."

"Yeah, why?" She tossed the pills into her mouth and swallowed them down with a swig of her coffee.

"Because I saw him this morning with Heather, too. Except he took off when I got close, and when I asked Heather if it was him, she said it wasn't."

"Hmm. Wonder what that means?"

"It means this class is going to be interesting, that's for sure."

"Well, we already knew that, considering who's going to be in it."

"Yes, I just hope they don't wind up killing each other."

The girl's arrived one by one, ready to hit the ground running. Caroline, then Heather, and the two older women who'd signed up for the class, Bonnie Bass, and Henrietta Harvey. I had to drag Heather away from poor Ellie

Jean Pruitt. She'd latched onto her in the main foyer of the library and started in on her about the dismal state of the library and how she was into reds and the reds would so brighten the look of the place.

"Heather, class will be starting any minute, and Ms. Pruitt here has a library to run."

"Oh, honey, I know that, but it's so dark and dingy, and my reds would add such a pop of color, don't you think?"

"I have to run over to the Abernathy house in a bit anyway, and I need to get some things done before I leave. I need to pick up something Mr. Abernathy left with his wife for a library board meeting," Ellie Jean said.

I practically yanked her away from poor Ellie Jean and into the conference room. The woman smiled at me as I waved and closed the door behind us.

"You don't have to be so rude," Heather said.

"We have a time line to follow, Heather, that's all."

Finally, after we'd all settled in and class started, Savannah made her grand entrance. And grand it was, plus totally intentional.

"I'm sorry I'm late," she said, bursting into the conference room as if everyone knew she'd be there.

Both Heather and Caroline gasped. Belle snickered, her headache apparently better.

"You better not leave now," I whispered to Belle.

A big grin stretched across her face. "And miss this little catawampus? No way, baby."

"You have the face of an angel and the soul of a sinner."

"My momma says that, too."

"Where do you think I got it?"

Heather pushed her chair back from the conference room table. "Lily Sprayberry, what were you thinking, inviting this… this hussy into here like this?" She shot out of her seat and marched to the door. "If she's here, I...I just can't be a part of this. You know what she did to me."

I whispered out of the corner of my mouth to Belle. "Soul of a sinner for sure." I cut Heather off before she left. "Heather, wait."

"Oh, for heaven's sake, don't pitch a fit because of me," Savannah said. "You think I need a class like this? Sweetie, I live in Buckhead. I have people that declutter and organize for me. I don't need to do it myself."

Except she just spent the last two weeks doing it at her parent's house, so that didn't really make sense, unless it was because her parents were paying for it and not her rich husband or in-laws.

I breathed a sigh of relief knowing she was leaving, but Belle's eyes about popped out of her head in utter disappointment. "What do you mean? You're signed up for the class."

She wiggled her designer purse and flung it over her shoulder. "Why would I waste my time drinking cheap sweat tea with —" She waved her hand across the room. "With women that hate me? If I'm going to do that, I'll just do it in town with my fake friends there. At least there I'll get a good cup of espresso."

Ouch. Millie's tea was by far the best in the south, and she definitely didn't deserve the criticism from Savannah, whose personality had gone well passed snooty to self-righteous in a hot minute.

"We'd love you to stay," Belle said, and I thought she actually meant it.

"Over my dead body, or better yet, hers," Heather said. "I cannot even consider staying if that hussy stays."

Savannah straightened her shoulders. "Why, I have a mind to—"

Heather pushed up her sleeves. "It's about time we do."

I jumped between them and stretched out my arms, locking my elbows just in case. "Come on already. We're adults. Let's act like it."

"I'm with Heather," Caroline said. "If Savannah thinks she can just waltz in here and act like she didn't try to sleep with my husband, well then—"

"He wasn't your husband at the time," Savannah said.

"I should have brought a bag of microwave popcorn," Henrietta said.

Bonnie dug in her purse. "I might have some in here somewhere." She picked out a bag of crackers, two packs of gum, a makeup bag, her wallet, and then finally huffed and said, "Oh, heavens," and dumped the bag's contents onto the table. After pushing the items around and not finding the popcorn bag, she sighed. "Nope, none."

"That's too bad. This cat fight deserves a good bag of microwave popcorn," Henrietta said.

We'd all watched Bonnie, surprised and bemused by her search for a bag of popcorn in her purse, and when she shoved the items on the table back into her bag, it brought us all back to reality.

Caroline stood and pointed her finger at Savannah. "Oh, darling, he's my husband now, and I'm warning you, you lay one gel nail on my man and you won't live to regret it."

Belle coughed.

"Is everything all right?" Ellie Jean Pruitt asked. She'd been moving the empty chairs away from the table to give us all some extra room when Savannah walked in.

"We're fine, Mrs. Pruitt." I turned to Savannah. "Maybe it's best you don't take the class."

"I never really planned on it. I just wanted to see how my two long lost friends would react when they saw me. But, of course, you can still show my parent's home tomorrow. I'll be there to let you in and then I'll leave so they don't pitch another hissy fit." She plucked a treat from the tray on the table, took a bite, made a scrunched up face and then set the treat back on the tray. "Oh, and Heather, you can have your sweet Austin back. I'm divorcing him. You'll love my sloppy seconds." She smiled at me, and as she walked out, said, "See you tomorrow, lovies. Ta ta."

Heather hollered after her. "He was my sloppy seconds first."

"That went well," Belle said and took a sip of her tea.

"That…that, well, I just can't use the kind of words I want because I'm a lady, but let me tell you, she's about as welcome in this town as an outhouse breeze," Caroline said.

That was probably one of the worst insults one could give a southern woman, and I thanked the Lord above Savannah wasn't there to hear it.

I stood staring at the other clients in the room. Bonnie and Henrietta gave each other a knowing glance. Ellie Jean fussed with the chairs, and Caroline and Heather shot daggers at me. I tapped my pencil on the conference room table, both to get everyone's attention and to focus my thoughts on how to start the class. "So, there are four key elements to decluttering and staging a home." I figured it was best to pretend nothing had happened and just move forward.

"That little hussy makes me so mad I could spit nails," Heather said.

"And to think she just walks in here like she never slept with our men," Caroline added.

"She didn't just sleep with my man, Caroline. She married him."

"Well, at least you found out before you married him. Imagine how that could have turned out," Caroline added.

"I couldn't marry him because he dumped me for her."

"Exactly. Look at me. I'll never know if my William slept with her for sure or not. He won't say, and now I'm married to him without knowing the truth." She fell into her seat and fanned her face with the packet full of papers I'd provided. "And heaven help her, if she even goes near my William, she won't see the light of day."

If the rest of my week went like the first fifteen minutes of class, heaven help me. "Ladies, how about we focus on why we're here instead of digging up the past?"

"Absolutely," Belle agreed. "What's done is done. Let's just move on. What do you say?"

"You would say that," Heather said. "The hussy never slept with your boyfriend."

"That's because she had several. Even Savannah would have had a hard time keeping up." Caroline said.

Bonnie hooted. "Ooh wee, she shoots to kill, don't she?"

Henrietta nodded. "Emm, hmm. Reminds me of myself back in the day."

I wanted to duck because I feared Belle would very likely chuck a scone straight at Caroline's face, and I was right in the line of fire. Only she didn't. It had to be because she hadn't slept the night before and was off her game.

I did my best to stop the fighting and regain control of my environment. I singled out Heather and Caroline, making eye contact with both of them. "Okay, that's enough. I've got a class to teach here, so if you two want to talk about this you're going to have to step out and do it elsewhere. The other women in this class didn't pay to listen to you two pitch fits about stuff that happened years ago."

"Oh, it's okay," Henrietta said. "They canceled my soap operas, so this is all kinds of fun for me."

Bonnie giggled. "For me, too. I haven't seen something this exciting in months, and I love me a good drama."

"Someone might could tell that one that just left that you can catch more bees with honey than vinegar. Her momma didn't do right by her, I can tell you that."

"Emm hmm," Bonnie said.

Belle bit her bottom lip to stop herself from laughing.

I had to admit, they were two little spitfires. I held back a giggle also. "Thank you for your ability to roll with things, ladies, I appreciate it, but this isn't the time of place for drama." I directed my next comments to my old friends. "So, take your pick ladies. Leave and trash talk, or stay and learn some valuable tools for your future. What's it going to be?"

They both grunted, crossed their arms over their chests and didn't budge. I assumed that meant they'd decided to stay.

We made it through the first day of class without any additional drama, and frankly, I was surprised. I begged the Lord and every deceased real estate agent in the heavens above to help me get through the next day when we all toured Savannah's parent's home. I wanted to finish the tour without any damages to the property, myself, or my clients.

Unfortunately, that prayer went unanswered.

CHAPTER 2

*B*elle and I sat at our desks, me trying hard to get real work done while she babbled on incessantly about the drama from the class. "Did you see the look on Savannah's face? Dear Lord, the way she stared at Heather, I thought nails would shoot right out of her eyeballs."

"'Smiling like a goat in a briar patch,' that's what my momma would say."

"Yes, she would, and she'd be right, too." She sat up in her chair and twisted her hair into a bun behind her head. "I honestly didn't think she'd behave that way. Savannah, I mean."

I flipped my chair around and faced her. "Me, neither. It was pretty petty of her and totally unnecessary."

"Exactly. I mean, why pour salt in the wound? We all know she won, so what was the point?"

"I don't know, but I'm going over there tonight, and I intend to ask her."

"Better you than me. I'm not sure I could be nice to her now."

"Really? You're kind of the one that started all of this. Maybe you should be the one to go?"

She dropped her jaw and gave me a wide-eyed stare as she pressed her hand against her chest. "What? I did not."

"Oh please. You totally did. When you found out she was coming back to town and wanted the help with her parent's house, you jumped on inviting her to the decluttering and staging class."

A slow smile moved across her lips. "Okay, so I did do that, but I didn't think it would be this horrible."

"Uh huh." I wiggled a finger at her. "I know you. You'd call an alligator a lizard if it'd win you a bet."

"True but not with you. You know me too well. I can't lie to you."

"I know, but still. You can't deny that was fun for you today."

"No, I can't deny that. I just feel bad you nearly got tarred and feathered having to bust up a cock fight but then again, you would have had Dylan to tend to those wounds."

"It was more like a group hen fight, but no, I'd have had Billy Ray Brownlee, a Band-Aid and a big glass of sweet tea."

"Sweet Billy Ray. He's older than dirt and completely uneducated in all things paramedic, but he's got a heart of gold, doesn't he?"

"He sure does."

"Honestly though, I was hoping the whole college thing would be water under the bridge. I kind of thought they could all move past it and things would be like old times, you know?"

The sadness in Belle's eyes surprised me. "Yes, I know. I miss that, too."

"Things will never be what they were, will they?"

"Nope, but that doesn't mean they can't be better, right?"

She smiled. "Right. I'm sorry I created this mess."

"Don't sweat it. Your intentions were honorable, and besides, I didn't stop you. "

She smirked. "As if that would even be possible, Miss Too Nice for Her Own Good."

~

After taking care of the rest of my clients and handling general real estate busy work, I picked up Bo and headed home. We ate dinner together, his on the floor and mine at the table, and I finished off the leftover scone I snatched from class. After he vacuumed the remaining scone crumbs off the floor, he bounded to the door to go for our nightly walk. In the beginning, doggy daycare wore my little guy out, but now, after a little nourishment, his second wind kicked in and his energy soared. Somewhere inside his non-stop growing body was a battery that never died. Ever.

Planning to stop at Savannah's and post some notes on various items throughout the house, I grabbed my bag along with Bo's collar controller. We walked over a mile as the sun slowly set to the west of us and turned around near the long out of business Pure gas station where Bo left his mark next to the old Pure sign.

I used the training I'd learned in class and directed him to come to me. "Bo Sprayberry, you shouldn't mark that. It's practically a historic monument."

He pushed his ears back as his little, sad eyes widened, and he barked.

I crouched down and rubbed his nose. "Don't you get sassy with me."

He licked my face, the sloppy, slimy underside of his tongue coating my face on the down lick.

"Ew, but thank you for the kisses."

His tailed wiggled back and forth.

We wandered like we had no plans over to Savannah's parent's house. When we got there Bo was so excited by the new smells, he marked every azalea bush lining the walkway up to the front porch.

Savannah answered wearing an old, stretched tank top with

a black workout bra underneath and a pair of baggy gray sweats. Even while we got the house in shape, she hadn't dressed down like that. She'd twisted her dark hair into a clip attached on the top of her head, and her eye makeup had smeared a little under her eyes. I wondered if she'd been crying.

"Hey girlfriend, come on in." She glanced down at my little monster who sat patiently by my side, his behind wiggling ferociously as his tail swept the front porch. She grimaced. "Oh, you brought a friend." She sniffled.

She'd definitely been crying.

"He can hang out in the backyard. He's not a digger, and he won't try to jump over the fence." I couldn't guarantee that, but I was at least ninety-nine percent sure.

She glanced at Bo again, and his tail wag whipped into high gear. "Perfect, I'll just meet you out back. That way he won't get any little dog prints all over the redone floors."

Bo thought he hit the jackpot in the backyard. Twice the size of ours, he took off running with a serious case of the zoomies. Just watching him wore me out.

I corralled the stick up notes and a pen from my bag and wrote out the features I wanted to highlight from our staging and decluttering. Realtors will recommend an entire house be staged but that cost a lot of money, and in small towns, that kind of money wasn't always an option. I preferred to focus on removing the clutter to create a clean, open space while making inexpensive updates that popped and pleased the eye. Open and airy sold homes, and in the older houses in Bramblett County where rooms interconnected only through walls or hallways, the best way to create the image of openness was by decluttering and painting.

We'd given the parlor, now called the living room—a term brought south from up north—an update with a fresh coat of light gray paint, so I stuck a note on the main wall and went from there. "So, class surprised me today. I didn't expect it to go like that."

"Are you referring to my part in it or theirs?" Savannah asked.

"Well, I'm here, so…"

"Bless their hearts, they just don't get it. I didn't steal Austin from Heather. He went willingly. No one can steal a man from a woman. The man decides for himself whether he wants to stay or go. I'm just tired of being the bad guy in all of it."

"Savannah, come on. Let's be real here. Of course you played a part in his decision. He didn't just decide to cheat on Heather alone. It takes two to do that."

She laughed. "Is it my fault that a man finds me attractive? That a man wants to spend time with me? It's not like I threw myself at him. A lady doesn't do that."

I had a feeling we didn't share the same definition of lady. "I guess from the outside it looks different."

"Even if I did steal him away, she should be grateful. Austin isn't the man Heather thinks. Why would I be divorcing him if he was?"

Savannah had been tight-lipped about the reasons for her divorce, and the curious girl in me really wanted the details. I couldn't help myself. "So, what's the story? What happened with you two?"

"Austin's a spoiled little rich boy that won't stand up to his parents. And honestly, if he can't be a man at home, how can I expect him to be a man in the real world? A woman like me needs a real man, not some little momma's boy who can't make a decision for himself without checking with his parents first."

I stuck another note on the book shelf where we'd removed most of the family photos and replaced them with old books from the attic and various knick-knacks from around the house. "I'm not sure I understand."

She fell onto the couch and groaned, clearly for dramatic

effect. "Sweetie, if a man can't stand up to his momma and daddy, he just isn't a man. You know that."

"So, you're divorcing him because he is a softy?" I placed a yellow sticky note on the top of the antique cedar trunk in the room now called the den.

"No honey, I'm divorcing him because his momma still tells him what to do, and his daddy controls my pocketbook. I told them it was time Austin and I handled our own finances. That man is twenty-eight-years-old and still gets an allowance. Can you believe that? I'm tired of having to run to his daddy every time he stuffs too many twenties into the belt of one of them floozies he—" She waved her hand. "I just can't talk about it." She grabbed a tissue from a box on the table and wiped her nose. "It's too painful."

Was she trying to tell me Austin was cheating on her with prostitutes? God bless. If that was true, Heather was lucky. "I'm sorry. I shouldn't have asked."

"It's okay." She wiped her nose again. "The worst part is when I went to his parents, they were so upset, they cut him off, and that ma—that boy doesn't have the guts to stand up to them. I can't live with someone like that." She sniffed. "I just can't."

"Is he trying to work things out or something?"

"As if I would ever even consider that. Why do you ask?"

"Dylan ran into him last night at Willy's. He said they talked a bit, and Austin mentioned something about a money situation."

"Austin's here? In Bramblett?"

"Apparently. You haven't seen him?"

She shook her head. "He's the last person I want to see. The last time we spoke, he threatened to kill me."

～

A typed note hung on the front door to Savannah's parent's house. "Had to meet with my attorney downtown. So sorry I can't be here for the excitement. Lock the door when you leave. Tootles. SE"

Belle's tone bled sarcasm. "Tootles? Is that how they speak in the big city?"

I shrugged. "How should I know?"

"You need to watch that Housewives show. Isn't there one filmed in the A-T-L?"

"I have no idea. I don't watch reality TV."

"That's my point. It's got to be better than those crime shows. You should branch out, add some variety to your life."

"I have a puppy. I don't have time for variety."

"How's my little nephew? I haven't seen him in almost a full day. I miss him."

"He's awesome. Getting bigger by the minute."

Caroline pulled up and parked her car on the side of the street. She rolled down the passenger side window and waved. "Hey, y'all. Is it okay if I park here?"

"Sure," I hollered.

Savannah's parents lived just two blocks from the main strip through town in an old Civil War era home. I would have given my left arm to buy that house, but the listing price I'd recommended to them was well above my budget. I had no need for a five-thousand square foot home anyway.

Caroline joined us on the wrap around front porch. Like my previous client's home, Mr. and Mrs. Armstrong's house had black shutters, but they'd recently been painted with a glossy shine that made them pop from the white wood planks. The differences though, were what made the Armstrong's house a saleable home. Myrtle was eighty-five-years-old when she was murdered a few months before, and she'd been unable to maintain the glory of her old home, but the Armstrong's had done their best to retain as much of the historic feel as possible. They'd kept the planks, or slats as some called them, wooden instead of replacing them with hardi-plank. They didn't cover up the brick columns that supported the home up from the ground like other homeowners had, and they left the azalea bushes lining the front of the house rather than replace them with smaller, easier to manicure shrubs. Mr. Armstrong loved his yard, and he spent practically every weekend outside trimming, raking, edging, snipping and clipping to keep it tidy and beautiful. And it was. His Crepe Myrtle trees, a rainbow of pastel pinks, whites, purples and reds, flourished in his yard and lined the driveway, shading the front right side of the big house. I hoped whoever bought the house would take care of the yard with similar gentle and loving hands.

I'd hung out at Savannah's house countless times growing up, and I'd never appreciated the old dark wood plank floors and the wood slatted panel walls in Savannah's bedroom, but now the creaking floors and the scuffed paneling added character, and I saw their value. I recognized and appreciated their history. I fell in love with the house in those two weeks I'd cleared and organized it, and unlike the Armstrong's, I couldn't imagine parting with such a treasure.

I plucked the note from the door and stuffed it in my bag. I didn't want it left out for a stranger to see. The last thing I needed was Savannah's parent's house being robbed because I'd left the note there. Crime didn't happen often in Bramblett County, but after Myrtle's death and the amount of people that went in and out of her home searching for the hidden money, I just didn't want to take any chances.

"Well, I for one am tickled she's not here," Caroline said.

"You and me both," Heather said, coming around the left side of the house.

"Bummer," Belle mumbled under her breath.

"Hush," I mumbled back, and then I smiled at Heather. "When did you get here?"

"A few minutes ago. I wanted to have a look in the back yard, see if that old Sweet Gum tree was still there. You know, for old time's sake."

"You mean the one we used to climb up in and talk for hours?" Caroline asked.

Heather nodded. "Those were good times, weren't they? Too bad Savannah had to go and ruin the memories by giving my boyfriend a taste of the promised land."

I sighed deeply and loudly, hoping to make a point. "So, a while ago Savannah contacted our office—"

Belle pointed her thumbs at her chest. "Yours truly."

"I stand corrected. Savannah contacted Belle and told her she'd be coming back to town to help her parents prepare their house for sale. She wanted to see if we could help her."

Belle nodded. "We'd been thinking about this class for some time, especially since Lily is certified in home staging, and I'll confess, I set it up even before telling Lily about Savannah coming to town."

Bonnie and Henrietta waddled up the drive, both of them breathless from the short walk from the road.

Bonnie gripped the porch railing with one hand and wiped her brow with the other. "For heaven's sake, you're slower than a jar of molasses, Henrietta."

"Now don't you go and get ugly, old woman." Henrietta latched onto the porch railing, too. "Lily and Belle here don't need us old biddies pitching a fit like the others did yesterday." She pointed to Heather and Caroline.

Belle chuckled.

Caroline blushed, but Heather dug her heels into the ground. "I had every right to be upset. Seeing Savannah Armstrong without warning like that, why, that was just horrible. I was so upset, I couldn't paint the rest of the day."

"Emmerson," Belle said.

Heather huffed and shot Belle a look that could kill. "I know that. I just refuse to say it."

"Okay then, let's start outside," I said. "Now, Henrietta and Bonnie, you might not know the Armstrong family, but Mr. Armstrong was very particular about his yard."

"Oh, I know them all right," Bonnie said. "I used to work at the hardware store, and Mr. Armstrong would come in every week and get himself some fertilizer and such." She nodded while examining the landscape. "Looks like we knew what we were selling."

We discussed the lawn and the importance of curb appeal when selling a home. Belle had a green thumb, but mine was black as the night, so she dug deeper into plants and flowers and what could grow where before we headed into the house.

I watched Heather and Caroline as their eyes wandered through the foyer. Caroline scratched and rubbed her arms, and if I remembered correctly, when she blinked a lot, like at that moment, that meant she was nervous. Heather's face stayed tight, nearly frozen without expression other than the slight up lift to her cheeks. I suspected she was less nervous and more annoyed to be in close proximity to some place her ex-boyfriend and his wife had been together.

"At least there aren't any happy family pictures," Heather said.

I ignored the obvious ugly intention in her tone. "We want potential buyers to feel like they could live in the home, not that someone else already lives in it."

Bonnie surveyed the area, running her fingers across a wood entry table. "I might could live here."

"I might could, too." Henrietta pointed toward the kitchen. "What kind of stove is there? I got one of those new electronic ones, but I can't cook a thing on it. It confuses me with all them fancy buttons."

"It's also one of those new electric ones," I said. "Let's work our way to the kitchen."

I noted several different key elements to staging and decluttering, and as we worked our way around the house, I removed each yellow note relative to the discussion. Once we made it through the first floor, we doubled back to the formal living room to discuss storage. "Once you've cleared the cluttered and determined what—"

Henrietta pulled the yellow note from the old cedar trunk. "You missed this one." She held it close to her glasses. "I can't read nothing on it though. Looks like chicken scratch to me, and besides, it's all blurry." She handed the note to Bonnie. "Can you read this?"

Bonnie stretched her arm out as far as it would go, dropped her glasses from the bridge of her nose to its tip, and read the note. "Store things you want to keep around but not have visible to onlookers in drawers and the like."

"So what kind of things you got stored in this here trunk?" Henrietta unlatched the trunk drawbolts and turned the key in the lock. She pulled the lid open. "Looks like it'd be the perfect place to—"

Belle gasped. "Oh, Lord."

Henrietta glanced into the trunk and screamed.

It was Savannah, and she was dead.

CHAPTER 3

The news of a dead body traveled fast, and in less than an hour most of the town had gathered on the front lawn and area surrounding the Armstrong home. A few brought coolers as they always did when something exciting happened in our small county. Nothing was off limits as cause for a celebration to the folks in town, and that included murder.

Belle squeezed my hand. "Just another average day in Bramblett County Georgia."

Based on the previous two dead bodies I'd found, she wasn't wrong. I desperately wanted to pick up Bo from doggy daycare and hide in my house for the rest of my life. "Belle Pyott, Savannah was our friend. Have some respect."

She grimaced. "I do, but you know how I get."

Some people cried in the face of tragedy. Belle however, did and said whatever she could to make light of it. Her defense mechanism wasn't just to protect herself, she also wanted to shelter and safeguard the people she loved. I apologized for jumping on her. "I'm a horrible friend sometimes."

She wrapped her arm around my shoulder. "You are not. You just found your third dead body in less than what, three months?

And like you said, she was a friend of ours. I was wrong to make light of it. I'm the one that should be sorry."

A tear rolled down my cheek. Get it together, Lily.

Dylan had arrived a few minutes after we'd called 911, and after getting the details from us, headed straight inside. A deputy secured the scene from the outside while another one managed the onlookers, or at least tried to. After what felt like hours, but was more like thirty minutes, the not-yet-defined man in my life stepped outside and signaled for the two of us to join him behind the yellow tape and on the front porch. Belle made some comment about special privileges, but I didn't hear the whole thing because I was too busy wiping my face and pulling myself together. I didn't want him to know I'd even come close to crying let alone already shed a tear. I didn't know why I felt the need to be tough around him, but nonetheless, that's how I felt.

"I'm going to get statements from the other ladies, but I wanted to talk with the two of you one more time before I do."

We both nodded. When he'd arrived, we gave him a quick run through of what happened, but nothing too detailed because he needed to get inside and manage the situation.

"Belle, why don't you run me through what happened again? Start from when you arrived to when I got here, okay?"

"Okay." She pursed her lips together. "Lily and I got here around the same time. Separate cars."

She spoke in short, direct sentences, totally un-Belle-like. I wondered if that was on purpose.

She waved her right hand toward the ground. "Waited here on the front porch for the others to arrive. Saw the note and—"

Dylan interrupted her. "Note?"

"Oh!" I swiveled around. "Where's my bag? I put it in there." I pointed to the front door. "Can I go get it?"

Dylan shook his head. "Let's wait until the coroner is finished, okay?"

I nodded.

"What did the note say?"

Belle responded. "That she had to meet with her attorney and to lock up when we left."

"She being Savannah I assume?"

She nodded. "Then we went in, and Lily began the class. Pointed out some of the stick up notes she'd left the night before, detailed the what and why for them, and then Henrietta saw one of them on the trunk and opened it."

The skin around the corners of her eyes bunched. "Oh, dear Lord, Savannah is dead." She clutched her stomach and bent over. "I'm going to be ill."

Reality just hit her. I grabbed hold of her. "You okay, honey? Do you want me to get Billy Ray?"

I didn't have to. Dylan clicked the little radio on his shoulder and asked for them to send him over. In the meantime, I guided Belle to the swing and gently sat her down. "You did good honey." I rubbed her back. "It's not easy, trust me. I know."

"I'll be back in a bit," Dylan said and headed back into the house.

She leaned back on the swing. "Don't make it move. Please, my breakfast might make a reappearance, and you know how much I hate that."

I knew how much everyone hated that, actually.

Billy Ray showed up with a cup of sweet tea, an ice pack wrapped in a cloth—something new to the mix—and a Band Aid. "Here you go Booboo, this ought to have your stomach feeling good as new right quick."

Belle took the drink and sipped it. "Thank you, Billy Ray. I don't think I need the Band Aid though. You can't put that on a broken heart."

Billy Ray frowned. "I know, but you keep it anyway. Might could use it sometime later. I got me a whole bag full of them anyway." He placed his hand on her shoulder. "I'm sorry 'bout your friend. I know you two was close once. It's hard to lose someone, no matter how close you were now, she meant something to you before, and that matters."

Dang it. Billy Ray flipped the tear switch on for both me and Belle, and the dam broke. Tears poured out from the both of us.

"Aw, now look what I gone and did." He shook his head and his shoulders drooped. "Here I am, trying to make you feel better, and I set you both to crying. Ain't no good at properly consoling a lady in despair now, that's for sure."

Belle finished the tiny cup of sweet tea and stood. She wrapped her arms around Billy Ray and squeezed him into a tight hug. "Billy Ray Brownlee, don't you go thinking that one bit. You are the master at making a lady feel better. My heart is already healing because of your kind words."

She'd hugged him with such force his eyes practically bulged from their sockets, but the smile on his face showed his relief. When she finally let go, he released a deep breath. I hoped she didn't crack one of the old man's ribs.

"Then why you got them tears rolling down your cheeks?"

We both wiped our faces. "Because that's what ladies do, Billy Ray," I said.

Belle wiped her face with the side of her hand. "Yes, we cry at everything."

He nodded. "Ain't that the truth. My sister, 'fore she passed, she cried at the drop of a hat." He went on to tell us a story about his sister who died when he was twelve. It made us both want to cry all over again, but we didn't because we knew that would make him feel bad. Instead, we listened and smiled, and then sent him on his way.

We waited for Dylan to come back out, but instead a deputy came by and told us he'd asked for us to wait with the other women from the class off the porch and near the side of the house. He directed us to a sectioned off area of the yard within ear shot of the crowd.

"All that blood," Henrietta said. "It might could take years to get that out."

Bonnie guffawed. "I got the perfect solution for that. My momma showed me once after Daddy cut the head off of a chicken and came in the house and plopped right down on the couch like he hadn't just done it. The blood got all over his shirt. She told him not to wear his Sunday clothes when he cut them heads off, but my daddy, he never did listen to what Momma said. All you got to do is spray a little club soda and laundry detergent on it, let it sit a spell, pat—don't rub 'cause rubbing just makes the blood get in them fibers—and keep on doing that until the blood comes out. Nothing to it."

"Blood? I didn't notice any blood anywhere," I said.

Both Henrietta and Bonnie stared at me like I'd lost my mind.

"You didn't?" Bonnie asked. "Blood was ever'where. Can't believe you missed it. You might could do with an appointment at that eye doctor. What do they call them?"

"Orthothamalgust?" Henrietta asked.

"Yeah, that one," Bonnie said. "Looks like you could use a pair of glasses."

"I recently had an eye exam with my ophthalmologist, and I'm all good." I made a point of accentuating the word ophthalmologist.

Belle giggled, and I asked her if she saw any blood.

She shook her head. "There was something red on the trunk and maybe a little red stuff on the note, but I can't be sure it was blood."

Caroline agreed. "I saw that too, but I'm not sure it was blood either."

"I saw it on a few of the yellow stick up notes you went over. Where'd you put those?" Henrietta asked.

"They're in my bag with the note from the door."

Heather tipped her head back and glanced toward the sun.

She sighed. "I'm fixin' to pop a blood vessel here. Are we ever going to be dismissed?"

"You got ants in your pants or something?" Henrietta asked.

Heather snarled. "I have better things to do than waste my time standing around here, that's for sure."

Heather's nostrils flared, and she stood with her feet shoulder width apart. Prime for a fight, I did my best to keep the peace. "I don't think it will be that much longer. Do you want me to see if Billy Ray can get us some sweet tea?"

"I don't need sweet tea. I need to get out of here."

The crowd next to us split in two, and Austin Emmerson marched through the middle of it, his face red, worry set in his eyes through the furrowing of his brows. "Where's Savannah? Someone said she's dead."

"Dear Lord, it's like Myrtle Redbecker's murder all over again. Only it's the husband and not the great-nephew this time," Belle said.

I glared at her.

"Sorry."

Austin pushed his way to our little group. "Lily, is it true? Is my wife dead?"

Heather bowed up like a hen going after the biggest rooster in the flock. "From the looks of her stuffed in that trunk, she couldn't be any deader."

Henrietta and Bonnie gasped.

"Ooh wee. That one's gonna sting," Bonnie said.

Austin stepped close to Heather and stuck his nose down into her face. "You want to do this right now? Right now?" He thrust back his shoulders and stuck his chin up. "Then come on, let's do it. I don't have anything to lose anymore."

She cowered, and all the spitefulness in her dissipated. "I…I…"

Dylan had perfect timing and broke up the possible fight before it went full throttle. "Austin, how about we step over here and talk?"

Austin stomped away, his hands flailing around him and his head jerking in all directions while Dylan remained calm and steady.

I chided Heather like an elementary school teacher. "That was completely out of line. You should be ashamed of yourself."

She fixed her eyes on me and snickered. "Well, I for one am not upset that that boyfriend stealer is dead. You just don't get it Lily. You have this perfect little life, all wrapped up in a sweet little bow. You don't know what it's like to have your future pulled out from under you."

She couldn't have been more wrong. I'd been there, just maybe not in the exact situation, but I'd been there. Dylan left me my sophomore year at the University of Georgia. I spent seven years focused on building a future for myself and forgetting about him—although that part never really happened—so yes, I got it. I just didn't think it was the right time to go into my sob story, and I'd moved on, like a person was supposed to do. Heather was too involved in her own pity party to listen anyway.

Belle spoke in a calm, soft voice. "Heather, news flash. This isn't about you. Austin dumped you eight years ago. Move on already."

Heather's face flushed. "Well, I've never!"

"You might ought to sometime. It's good for ya," Bonnie said.

Heather clenched both fists. "I do not have to stand here and take this from the likes of you." She flipped around and bumped into a deputy.

"Going somewhere?" he asked.

"Yes, I have a job, and a career. I am an artist, and I have a painting to finish."

"Ma'am, Sheriff Roberts hasn't given permission for any of you to leave. I suggest you hold on a bit until he does."

Heather glared my direction. "Can you talk to your boyfriend? I don't have time for this."

"I, uh…"

Dylan squeezed my arm. "I got this." He held up a red zipper sweat jacket. "This belong to any of you?"

Heather swung her arm out to grab the jacket, but Dylan yanked it back. "That's mine."

"When did you have it on last?"

She stuck out her chin. "Yesterday morning. It was a bit chilly when I left, so I went inside again right quick and grabbed it from the coat rack. Why?"

Dylan whispered something to the deputy.

"Ma'am, I'd like you to come with me to the station."

Heather dug her heels into the ground. "I'm not going anywhere until you tell me what's going on."

Dylan used his calm but authoritative voice, the soft, low one that accentuated his southern drawl. "We've got some questions for you, Heather, and it's best they're asked at the station. I'll be there soon. Just go and sit tight, okay?"

She pitched a fit bigger than the state of Texas. "Why am I going to the station? Do you think I had something to do with that…that…with Savannah's murder? What's going on? I need a lawyer. Someone get me a lawyer."

"You're within your rights to have an attorney present at the time of questioning if you so desire, ma'am, and we can make arrangements for you to contact one at the station. Now, if you'll just come with me." The deputy held onto her arm and all but dragged her to his car.

"Well, I am most definitely going to get myself an attorney. This is police brutality, that's what it is. I am a victim here." She screamed so everyone could hear her. "A victim!"

Henrietta shook her head. "Oh, that can't be good."

"If she did it, then maybe her paintings will sell, and she'll die one of them martyrs or what you call them. You know, like that famous guy that cut his nose off did."

"It was Van Gogh and it was his ear, not his nose," Belle said.

"Yeah, that's what I said. His ear. Cut it off so his paintings would sell. Smart man right there."

That wasn't exactly how the story went, but I knew Belle wasn't going to fill her in when she shook her head and turned away.

"What's going on?" Caroline asked Dylan.

He'd been distracted for a moment by the two older women. He smiled at them and then at Caroline. "One of the neighbors said they saw someone outside the house last night wearing a red jacket with a hood." He flicked his head toward the sheriff's vehicle with Heather in the back. "We found that in the house."

"Austin is wearing a red jacket," I said.

Dylan nodded. "He's headed to the station also. Another one of my deputies is taking him. Quietly, I hope."

William Abernathy arrived and hurried over to Caroline. "Honey, what's going on? Are you okay?"

"Oh, William, it's just terrible. Awful." She wrapped her arms around him and fell into him. He held her tight. "Savannah, she's dead. My old friend. Someone killed her."

She laid it on as thick as the sap dripping from a Georgia oak tree, and William fell for it completely.

"Why, I'm just devastated," she said. "I can't believe she's dead."

Bonnie coughed. "You can't? I recall you threatening her in class yesterday."

Henrietta nodded. "Yeah, I recall that, too. And you pitched a hissy fit at Millie's yesterday afternoon."

"That's right, she sure did. One with a tail on it," Bonnie agreed. "Thought you would pull that poor girl's hair out right there."

When a southern woman pitched a hissy fit with a tail on it, that meant it was serious.

Caroline's face reddened. "It wasn't…it wasn't like that."

"What are they talking about?" I asked.

"Why, she was arguing something fierce with that dead girl at Millie's yesterday after class," Bonnie said.

"Threw her drink in her face, she did," Henrietta said.

Bonnie made a tsk, tsk sound. "Waste of money it was, too."

I heard a slight chuckle from Dylan, but he kept it soft and under his breath, so I hoped the others didn't hear it, too.

"Waste of good sweet tea, too. The best in the state," Henrietta said.

Dylan stepped between the women and directed his attention toward Caroline. "You had a confrontation with Savannah yesterday?"

She lowered her eyes and stared at the ground. "Yes…no, I mean, it wasn't…it wasn't like that. We had words, but that was it."

He raised an eyebrow. "Words that involved throwing your drink on her?"

"And threats," Henrietta said.

"What kind of threats?" Dylan asked.

"She said something about that hussy had better keep her filthy paws off her man or she wouldn't see the light of day because this girl ain't no softy like Heather." Bonnie coughed. "Or something like that."

William ran his hand through his hair. "Caroline, did you really do that?" He dropped his hand and turned in a circle. "What were you thinking?" He paced around the group of us standing there.

"It's not like they're saying, William. I promise. I just…I just didn't want her coming between us. I didn't want her ruining what we have." She burst into tears. "I just don't know what's come over me lately. I'm just a hot mess about everything." She buried her face into William's chest and sobbed.

He tilted her head back and kissed her gently on the forehead. "Why would you think she'd ruin what we have? Come on Caroline, nothing happened back then, and it certainly won't happen now."

"Nope, it sure won't 'cause she's deader than a doornail now," Henrietta said.

The side of Dylan's mouth twitched. Inappropriateness aside, Henrietta and Bonnie were a hoot.

Dylan patted William on the shoulder. "Would you mind bringing your wife to the station? I'd like to ask her a few questions. I'll be done here in a bit."

"Do you really think that's necessary? It was an innocent argument. She's been under a lot of stress lately. Sick practically every day, exhausted. She's just not herself. She didn't mean anything by it."

"I'm sure she didn't, but I'm going to need to talk with her anyway, buddy."

"Is she under arrest?"

Caroline shivered, and her teeth clattered. "Am I going to jail? I can't go to jail. I have a hair appointment this afternoon. I'm getting a foil. You know how hard it is to schedule those?" She grabbed at her hair and pulled. "Look at my roots. They're a hot mess. I can't go on like this much longer. Please, don't make me miss my appointment. William, make him understand." She buried her face into his chest again.

"It's just a few questions, that's all." He glanced at me and mouthed. "We'll catch up later, okay?"

"Are we dismissed?" Henrietta asked.

Bonnie groaned. "I sure hope so. I'm pooped. All this excitement has got me needing a nap." She yawned and started a chain reaction for the rest of us.

"I could use some of that sweet tea Billy Ray's got," Henrietta said.

"You don't need no sweet tea. You're just looking for a date to bingo next week," Bonnie said.

Henrietta stiffened her torso and smirked. "A girl's gotta do what a girl's gotta do."

That time Dylan couldn't hold in his laughter. "You two are dismissed, but I don't want you leaving town any time soon, you hear me?"

Henrietta scooted up close to Dylan and patted his behind. "Sheriff, I don't have any plans of leaving a place where you are any time soon." She winked and scooted off.

Belle and I busted out laughing while Dylan just shook his head and walked away.

Belle whispered in my ear. "You going to let that old woman hit on your man like that?"

I smiled. "Honey, one day I hope to have half the spunk of that old woman."

"If you get even a quarter of it, it'll be a miracle."

We drove back to the office knowing Dylan would be in touch when he had the opportunity. Granted, we both were a bit shell shocked, but as we walked down the street, it hit us like a meteor falling onto our heads.

Belle kept shaking her head over and over. "I can't believe she's dead. It just seems so surreal. Savannah's dead."

"I know. I can't either. All these memories just keep flashing through my mind, you know? Like the time we all went camping at the lake? Remember that?"

"Which time? We did that every summer of high school."

"True, but that one time when we almost caught the woods on fire? That's the time that keeps coming back to me. We all could have died then."

She laughed. "Bless her heart, Savannah wasn't the sharpest tack in the box, was she? She could have gone down in history for destroying most of the state of Georgia all over again."

I laughed, too. "Who starts a fire in the middle of a woods full of pine trees when it's a hundred degrees out and hasn't rained in a month?"

"Savannah, apparently."

"Yeah, and then she runs screaming like it wasn't her fault."

Belle blew air from her nose. "That was kind of a theme in her life, wasn't it?"

"What?"

"Nothing being her fault."

I glanced at her. "Yes, but no matter what she's done, nothing was bad enough for her to deserve this."

"I know. And honestly, I don't even know what happened to her. I saw her in that trunk, and I just couldn't look at her. I had to look away."

"I couldn't either, but I don't remember any blood. I know you said there was blood or something on the sticky note, but I don't think that was blood. If she'd been killed in a way that made her bleed, wouldn't we have seen some on her? I can't stand the sight of blood, so I know I'd remember that." I tapped a pencil on my desk. "Dylan's going to have to bring me my bag soon. I need my laptop and planner to get anything done, and that note is in there. I'd like to see it."

"You have a desktop, you know."

"I know, but my planner is my world. Everything's in there. I'm basically crippled without it."

"Honey, you need to get with the modern world. Digital is the way to go. There's this thing called a calendar on your phone, and a place for reminders and notes. You should use those."

"I don't like those. You can't see everything in one spot, and you have to switch apps. It's hard on a Type A person like me."

"It's got to be rough living inside your head."

"I find it comforting most of the time."

"Except when someone takes the Lilybit Bible."

"Except then."

"I'm sure he'll bring it by once he's free, but he's probably taken the notes as evidence or something."

"Probably, but maybe he'll let me see them."

"I'm sure he will," she said.

"He'll tell me how she was killed, too."

"I'm not sure I want to know. It was bad enough finding her. Seeing her squished into that trunk like that? Lord, it doesn't matter what that girl did, she did not deserve to die that way."

"No, she didn't."

"This is going to sound totally inappropriate, but I'm hungry. Do you want to go grab something at Millie's? My treat."

"You know what? That sounds like a good idea. I'm not going to get much done right now anyway, and my momma always says 'food heals a wounded heart'."

"Well, my heart is wounded and starving, so food is definitely on the menu."

We walked over to Millie's Café for an iced coffee and a sandwich. I also had an ulterior motive. I wanted to find out what I could about the confrontation between Caroline and Savannah the day before.

The line wasn't long, and I was surprised to see Ellie Jean Pruitt at the end of it.

She saw us and gave me a hug. "Oh heavens, I heard the news." She hugged Belle, too. "You two must be a mess."

Belle nodded. "A little. It's just shocking, really."

I mustered up a half smile, but that was the best I could do. "It's been a rough day, that's for sure."

"I told my Faith, and well, she was beside herself."

"How is Faith?" I asked.

She waved her hand. "Oh, thank you for asking. She's just sweet as a peach. She lives off in Tennessee now. Got married a few years ago to an accountant, and he took her miles away from me." Her eyes narrowed a bit, and had I not been looking directly at them, I probably wouldn't have noticed. "But she's happy as a clam."

"That's wonderful."

Millie came out and handed Ellie Jean a bag. "Here you go, Ellie Jean. You tell them volunteers over at the library I'll give them a ten percent discount on lunches if they come in twice a week, okay?"

Ellie Jean smile. "Will do, Millie, and thank you." She waved to all of us as she walked through the door and left.

We placed our order with Millie, who shouted it to her kitchen staff and poured us fresh glasses of iced sweet tea while we waited. We didn't mention that we'd ordered iced coffees and drank the tea instead. With Millie, if she didn't get the order exactly right, you took what you got anyway. Complaining never did any good. In fact, sometimes it got you grounded from her café for weeks at a time. Neither Belle nor I wanted to take that risk. We lived for her caffeinated drinks.

She pulled out a chair and sat with us. "You two must be emotionally drained."

"Just a bit," Belle said.

Millie leaned toward us and whispered, "You know, it doesn't surprise me that Savannah was murdered. She shouldn't have come back to Bramblett County in the first place. With her reputation and the way she treated people, something horrible was bound to happen."

I sipped my tea and enjoyed the icy sensation as it slid down my throat. I didn't realize I was so thirsty. "Nobody deserves to die because of their reputation, Millie."

"Oh, I agree, but this ain't about what's right or wrong. People get what's coming to them no matter that. I sure hope that boyfriend of yours is talking to Caroline Abernathy because after what I saw yesterday, why that girl would be on the top of my suspect list." She sat back in her chair and nodded. "Let me tell you, I've seen women fight before, but the look on Caroline's face?" She shook her head. "I've never seen that kind of look before. It was pure evil."

Belle cocked her head. "Aren't you being a bit extreme, Millie?"

"I beg your pardon, but I do not do extreme. I call it as I see it. Go ahead, ask around. Anyone that was here yesterday will tell you the same thing. Caroline Abernathy threatened to kill Savannah, and I believe she would have done it right there had we all not been there watching."

I patted Millie's arm. I didn't want her upset with either of us, but I also didn't want her making a bad situation worse by spreading gossip. "I'm sure Dylan will do what needs to be done, and I appreciate you giving me the information. I'll make sure to get it to him."

"Thank you. And you tell him if he needs me to come to the station and be a witness, I can do that. I want to keep this county safe from murderers."

Her kitchen person handed Belle our bags and we walked back to our office.

"That Millie sure puts the icing on the cake in the drama department, doesn't she?"

I laughed. "Just a bit."

"I sure hope I never have to be on the tail end of that."

"You and me both, or anyone we love."

❧

"Bo, stay." He stuck like glue to my side. I wanted to do my happy dance, but I couldn't ruin the moment.

"He's doing great," Dylan said.

I pushed out my bottom lip. "Hey, I'm doing pretty great too, don't you think?"

He kissed my forehead. "You're doing fantastic. You're going to be an amazing mom."

The air filled with an awkward silence and thickened so much I nearly choked on it.

"Someday, Little Bean. Not soon, but some day." He laughed. "You're actually starting to sweat. That's funny."

I released Bo to go the dog park, and Dylan and I walked behind him. "No, it's not funny. I am so not ready to be a mom."

"Well, for one, you're not married, and we both know your mother would tan my hide if anything like that ever happened between us."

"Tan your hide is putting it mildly. You'd be dog food, and not the premium kind."

He winced. "Ouch. Your mom loves me."

"Loved. You're going to have to win her over again, and good luck with that by the way. You broke her baby's heart. That's an unforgivable sin in her book."

"But you forgave me."

I elbowed him in the side. "I'm working on it."

"Well then, I best try harder to make it happen."

"You could start with giving me back my bag. I'm useless without it."

"One, you're not useless without it. There are many uses for you sans your bag, and two, it's in my car. I'll give it to you when we leave."

I tipped my head back and raised my hands to the sky. "Thank you, God." I smiled at Dylan. "So, what happened with your interviews? Obviously, no one was arrested because the town gossip train hasn't reached me yet."

He nodded. "No, no arrests, but we're headed that direction. Matt's working on a few things, and we're putting the timeline of the last few days together."

"Shouldn't you be at the station doing that now?"

"I should, yes. I just wanted to come see you for a minute, tell you I'm probably going to be busy for the next few days, and I might not see you much until this case is wrapped up."

"I understand. I'm worried about Caroline. She was pretty shaken up earlier."

"She calmed down a bit at the station. William knows how to handle her."

I angled my head and scrunched my eyebrows together. "Handle her?"

He waved his hands in front of his chest. "No, no, I mean, he knows how to...to help her relax, to calm down. She admitted she's been on edge since seeing Savannah, for the last few weeks actually, and that she might have overreacted at Millie's."

"Do you think she could have killed her?"

"Why don't you tell me what you think."

"It's just a rumor, about Savannah and William, but there's always a bit of truth to every rumor, so, I guess I can see why she'd be upset."

"Even after all this time?"

"Yeah, that's the part I struggle with. I mean, sure, a year after the rumor started, maybe it's justifiable to still be upset, but they're married now, and they have been for a while, so I'm not sure why she's got a bug up her behind about it all of a sudden." I pushed a dangling curl from the side of my face. "I don't think it's reason enough to kill someone though, you know?"

"People have killed over smaller things."

"That's true. Happens on TV shows a lot."

He chuckled.

"Well, it does." I kicked a rock off the path as we walked up to the dog park. "Heather though, I'm a little concerned about her. She's still so angry, and there's a..." I didn't know how to describe what I saw in Heather's eyes when we found Savannah. "I don't know exactly. Maybe spite, or vindictiveness, something like that is brewing inside her. Whatever it is, it's not healthy." I picked up another rock and threw it behind me. "What did she say about her jacket? How did it get in Savannah's house?"

"She doesn't know. She said the last time she had it on was

yesterday morning. She put it on that morning, wore it to your class and doesn't remember wearing it after that. She thinks she left it there, or somewhere between the library, her parent's store and home. She's not sure."

"So, basically she conveniently forgot?"

"Basically, yes."

"Did she say where she was last night? Does she have an alibi?"

"Lily, this is an official investigation. We really shouldn't be talking about any of this. I don't want you involved, you know that especially after what happened with the Redbecker case."

My posture involuntarily stiffened. "What? But I'm already involved. I found the body. Well, I was one of the people that found the body."

"Yes, and that should be the extent of your involvement. You were nearly killed the last time you got involved in a murder investigation. I can't take that risk again. I don't want to lose you."

We stood outside the dog park's gate and watched the dogs play. I gripped the fence, and the veins in my hands bulged. "You can't lose me, but you'll gladly dump me when you're ready to move onto the next phase of your life."

He clutched the fence, leaned forward and then dropped his head and shook it. "I can't believe you just said that."

I couldn't believe I'd said it either. I didn't know where it came from. I guess I still felt threatened by our history, by his up and leaving me in college. "Well, I said it, so you should believe it." What was wrong with me? Why was I acting like a teenager?

He angled his body toward me and moved into my personal space. "Lily, I told you, I'm in this for good."

I couldn't look at him. I wanted to, but I knew if I did, I'd either kiss him or cry, and neither of those options sounded like the right choice, so instead I just watched an ant colony work their butts off for their queen, moving dirt around like the little minions they were.

"Lily, look at me." He used a finger to angle my chin toward him. "I'm not going anywhere. I promise you."

I swallowed. He couldn't really promise that. He'd already done that years ago, and he did go somewhere. Away from me. "May I have my bag, please?"

"Really? Is that how you're going to handle this?"

I called my dog. "Come on, Bo. Time to head home." He bounded over to the fence, and I opened the gate to let him out. I glanced up at Dylan. "I'll meet you at your car."

"Unbelievable." He took off jogging toward the parking lot.

Belle sat on my back patio with my monster-sized puppy on her lap as I filled her in on my situation with Dylan. "Girl, you haven't got the sense God gave a goose, and a dumb one at that. What were you thinking?"

"I wasn't thinking, I guess. I don't know. The words just came out, and once they did, I couldn't stop them."

"Or something."

"So, what do I do?"

"I'll tell you what you do. You get all gussied up, and you go over to Dylan's house, and you tell him you're sorry."

"I can't do that."

"Why not?"

"Because I don't think I'm sorry. I think I actually meant what I said. I don't trust that he won't up and leave me if some better job comes along or if he decides he doesn't want to be in Bramblett County anymore."

Either God planned an intervention, or Dylan had perfect timing, I wasn't sure which was the case, but nonetheless, he texted me.

"I need an official statement from you tomorrow, please. You can talk to one of my deputies. And I shouldn't be telling you this, but I trust you'll keep it private, the red on the sticky notes wasn't blood. It was paint."

Belle's phone dinged shortly after mine. "I need to give my statement tomorrow."

"So do I. And the red stuff on the sticky notes wasn't blood."

"What was it?"

"Paint."

CHAPTER 4

*D*ylan was at the station when I arrived. I didn't know what to say, so I just waved like he was some casual acquaintance I'd see at the coffee shop or walked past on my way to work. The deputy at the front desk had another deputy—we had a lot of deputies for a small county, but that wasn't uncommon in Georgia—escort me to the conference room back by Dylan's office. That's where I saw him. The deputy told me to have a seat and said someone would be with me to take my statement soon.

He kept his sentences short and to the point, and I wondered if he was agitated with me personally, or if that was just the way he was. I couldn't help but think he knew something had happened between me and his boss.

My mother's voice played in my head. "The world doesn't revolve around you, Lilybit. Get over yourself."

Dylan stepped into the room a few minutes later. When I looked up and into his eyes, my heart crashed into my stomach. "Oh, hi."

He placed a vanilla file folder, a pen and a mini recording device on the large table and sat across from me. "I'll make this as quick as possible."

"Okay." That wasn't what I wanted to say. I wanted to say I was sorry, and that I loved him, but the words stuck in my throat like a lump of bread, and I swallowed them back so I wouldn't choke on them.

He asked me a series of questions, all official and without any hint of emotion. I answered them in the same tone, doing my best to pretend he wasn't himself but some random deputy sheriff I had no history or connection to. When he finished, I asked if I could ask him some questions.

He leaned back in his chair. "This is an active investigation, and I'm not at liberty to share the details, but sure, you can give it a shot. I'll answer what I can."

Great. He wanted to play it like that. "There wasn't any blood at the scene. How was Savannah killed?"

"We've got a rush on the autopsy report, but the unofficial cause of death is asphyxiation from strangulation."

I cringed. What a horrible way to die. "Oh."

"We noted signs of petechiae on her neck, which was our first indication of strangulation. The coroner agrees, but we have to wait for the official report to confirm."

"What is petechiae?"

"They're like small bruises on the skin. Broken blood vessels really. In cases like this, they're typically seen on the neck and are caused from the pressure of the choke hold."

"So, the person that killed her did it with his bare hands?"

"Or hers."

"You think it was a woman?"

"I'm not saying it was a woman or a man."

"Do you have any suspects?"

"I'm not at liberty to say."

"Seriously?"

"I don't want you involved in this Lily."

"You don't really get a say in what I'm involved in."

"In this case, I do. I'm the sheriff."

Oh, yeah. I'd forgotten that little detail. I straightened in my seat. "It doesn't matter. I'm sure you're considering the same people I am."

That piqued his interest. "And who would that be?"

"I'm not at liberty to say."

The side of his mouth twitched, but I forced myself to look away because I wasn't going to let it get to me. No way. Not again. I hoped.

"Fair enough, but I mean it, stay out of my investigation, Lily."

I stood. "Yes, Sheriff Roberts." I headed toward the door.

He followed behind me and grabbed my arm. "Lily, wait."

I turned around, jerked my arm away and glared at him.

"Can we talk later? Please?"

"I'm sorry, Dylan. Not yet." I opened the door and forced myself to walk out of the building with my head held high.

❧

I didn't cry the whole drive to class. When I got there, Ellie Jean greeted me with another big hug. I didn't recall her being so sweet in high school, but her attention and affection was exactly what I needed.

"Sweetie, you look like something the cat drug in. You sure you're up for this today? Maybe you should cancel? I can tell the ladies it's off for the day and send them home."

"No, it's okay, but thank you. I need to do this. I'll be fine once I have some coffee and a bit of food." That's when I realized I'd forgotten to pick up the food at Millie's. "Well shoot. I forgot the order at Millie's." I set my bag and box down. "I need to run over there. Would you mind putting my stuff in the conference room? I don't want to leave it here in the way."

She picked up my things. "It's not a bother at all. You go on now and get yourself something, and don't worry a bit about this. I'll get the room set up." She peeked in the box. "I might could put these out for the ladies if you'd like?"

I breathed a sigh of relief. "That would be wonderful, Ellie Jean, thank you so much." I hugged her one more time and made a quick run to Millie's.

Millie's line hit the end of the block. I settled in behind a group of three older men, regulars who showed up every morning for coffee and biscuits. They nodded their hello and went back to their discussion.

The man with the long white beard that reminded me of Santa Claus, spoke first. "Sheriff needs to get a handle on the crime in this town. You ask me, bringin' him on wasn't smart. Murder rates gone up ever since he came on. Maybe he's got something to do with it?"

I bit my tongue.

"Don't think so. I know his pa. He ain't the kind of boy that kills just to look good. 'Sides, Myrtle Redbecker? Her murder, that wasn't him. That was one twisted tale right there."

I angled myself toward the street. My face was plastered all over town. If they actually paid attention, they'd have to know I was Myrtle's realtor, and I was involved in the whole situation from the start, and I preferred to remain anonymous at that moment.

The larger man wearing faded tan overalls, said, "Word is the dead girl had a bit of a reputation, if you know what I mean. I'm not saying she got what was coming to her, but you play with fire, you gone get burned. You hear what I'm sayin'?"

The men nodded, and Santa Claus's twin spoke again. "If I were the sheriff, I'd have a talk with the husband. You got a lady cheatin' like that, you're gonna have one ticked off husband, and there ain't no telling what a man can do when he finds out his wife ain't been faithful."

I loved living in a small community, but I hated how stories were twisted. I realized it happened everywhere, but in a small place like Bramblett County, where everyone pretty much knew everyone, the damage had a greater impact. Savannah might have cheated on Austin, I didn't think so, but I didn't know, but according to her, that wasn't the cause for her decision to divorce him, and rumors like that did nothing but make the situation worse.

I couldn't keep my mouth shut. I flipped around and poked my finger into fake Santa Claus's chest. "Actually, that's not what happened, and you should be ashamed of yourself for spreading rumors and speaking ill of the dead."

The men stepped back, so I stepped forward. "Savannah Emmerson was my friend, and I was with her shortly before she died. She was not the one cheating on her husband. You might could do yourself some good by keeping your mouth shut. Shame on you. At your age, a man like you should know better."

Millie came outside and took orders and the man in overalls hollered to her. "Hey Millie, we're gone take a seat over yonder." He pointed to the empty table near the edge of the windows connected to the store next to the café. "Away from this little spitfire right here." He wrapped his arm around me and whispered. "You done good honey, your momma would be proud," and then he hollered back to Millie, "You get to us when you can, you hear?"

She waved them off, and they headed to their seats. Millie caught my eye and winked. "Hey honey, I've got your stuff on the counter waiting for you. Go on in and grab it. You can pay me later."

I smiled, proud of myself for standing up for my friend and setting the record as straight as I could, knowing as much as I did. I walked past Millie, said, "Thank you," grabbed my bag and headed back to the library.

I considered the potential suspects on my brief walk back to the library. Austin, of course, was my number one suspect because like Santa Claus said, the spouse is always considered a suspect, and in real life, not on the TV shows, more times than not they're the ones that committed the crimes. Plus, Dylan said the neighbor saw someone in a red jacket outside of Savannah's house the night before we found her, and Austin had a red hoodie. Yes, Heather did also, and it was found inside the Armstrong's house, and I couldn't let that go.

I slowed my gait to give myself more time to think. I doubted the ladies would care if we started right on time, anyway.

Savannah did have a reputation, and her arrival back in town shocked both Caroline and Heather. Though we'd all been close growing up and in college, except Savannah after the Austin incident, of course, we all went our separate ways once we graduated. Belle and I obviously stayed best friends, our bond growing closer with the launch of our real estate business, and Caroline and Heather, from what I understood, had stayed best friends, too, but seeing Heather with William, and William taking off, and then Belle saying she saw them together also, well, that added a layer to things that made me wonder if Caroline and Heather's friendship wasn't in some kind of turmoil, and if Heather was capable of things I couldn't imagine.

Caroline and William married, and they'd taken over William's parent's corn maze and pumpkin patch. They'd established themselves in the community, whereas Heather never quite recouped from her break up with Austin. She'd expected to be Mrs. Austin Emmerson and spend her days living the good life, playing tennis and painting her time away somewhere other than Bramblett County. That hadn't happened. Instead, she still lived with her parents and worked at her store while trying to pan her paintings off to local small businesses. She hadn't dated in years, though I really couldn't judge her for that, or for any of it, for that matter.

It surprised me to see Caroline react to Savannah the way she had and to hear she'd pitched a fit at Millie's, and even alluding to killing her if she came near William was over the top.

Heather's disdain was at least partly justifiable, even if it was time to move on, but Caroline never had any proof of a relationship between William and Savannah, so, like I told Dylan, I struggled with thinking she'd actually kill Savannah over it, though I couldn't come to terms with why she was still so upset. She claimed her emotions were on overdrive, but that in and of itself was a bit unbelievable.

The only thing that stuck with me was what my momma always said. "There was always a little truth to a rumor". I wondered if Caroline knew something she didn't want anyone else to know? I kept Caroline on my mental list of suspects for that reason. A person didn't react the way she had without justification, or at least a belief of justification, and until I found out otherwise, she would stay on my list.

The three suspects on my list were all people I'd once been close to, and I just didn't want to think any of them capable of killing Savannah Emmerson.

I made it back to the library and saw Heather chatting with Ellie Jean, or Heather chatting at her, actually, and one of them—not Heather—showed signs of uncomfortableness. Heather leaned in toward Ellie Jean and she leaned out, almost backing up while she spoke at her. Her arms were crossed over her chest, and I'd learned in my business communications class that was a clear sign that someone had closed themselves off or felt the need to protect themselves from the person near them. The urge to intervene took over, and I set Millie's goodies down and stepped into their conversation.

"Hi, ladies. Ellie Jean, thank you so much for helping me this morning." I nodded to Heather. "Would you mind taking the bags from Millie's to the conference room for me?"

"Oh, honey, of course, but I was just explaining to Ellie Jean here how a few of my paintings would be lovely in the library, and especially in the conference room." She spread her arms out and scanned the room. "As my meemaw used to say, you can't make no silk purse out of a sow's ear, but at least the reds would add a pop of color to these dreary walls, and they'd brighten up that sad looking conference room for sure. I've mentioned how I'm into reds, right?"

"You might have," Ellie Jean said.

"Heather, I'm sure Ellie Jean would have to discuss this with the library board for any kind of decision right, Ellie Jean?"

She nodded. "Oh, yes. I am just the head librarian. I don't make financial or décor decisions at all, but I'll be sure to tell the board about your paintings, Heather. I saw one at my doctor's office the other day. They're quite lovely." The way she emphasized lovely made me question her honesty.

"Well then, I think I'll just have me a little conversation with the board myself," Heather said. "It's so dreary in this here library, I can't imagine anyone feels good when they leave here. I know I sure don't."

Oh my. Talk about hitting a woman where it hurt. Libraries were Ellie Jean's life, especially since her daughter had moved away. She mumbled something about painting by numbers kits under her breath, but I couldn't quite hear her.

Heather leaned toward her. "What did you say, Ellie Jean?"

"Oh, nothing dear. I was just mumbling to myself."

"Okay then, how about we head to class?" I heaved the bags into my arms and nudged Heather along. "We've got a lot to catch up on."

Heather followed, though unwillingly from the sound of her stomping. "I am so behind on my to do list, what, after being brought in for questioning for Savannah's murder and all. I can't believe the nerve of Dylan Roberts doing that to me." She flung her hair and huffed. "Now, I don't know if I'll ever catch up with this class taking up even more of my precious painting time. I'm not even sure I should be here. I mean, it's not like this is important anyway. I was just doing you a favor by attending."

I walked into the conference room without saying a word to her.

Belle and the rest of the group had already arrived and of course, the conversation focused on Savannah's murder. All of them except Caroline, who sat in utter silence, a dazed expression on her face.

"The sheriff called me in for a statement," Bonnie said. "And I thought he was going to arrest me right then and there."

"Oh Bonnie, you're a hot mess. Why would that man arrest you? You didn't do nothing wrong," Henrietta said.

"Oh, I know that. I was just hoping he'd put the handcuffs on me." She winked.

Belle choked on her bottled water.

"Now don't go acting like that around here. You know our teacher is the sheriff's girl. You don't want to get an F in class, do you?" Henrietta asked.

I set the bags down and placed the treats onto the plates for everyone to access. "It's okay, Bonnie. We're not giving grades in class, and I'm not dating the sheriff anymore."

Heather flicked her long, red hair. "Well that's interesting news. So, Dylan's available now?"

"Oh no, that ain't right," Henrietta said.

Belle thrust her palm out toward Heather's face. "Oh, sweetie, do not go there."

Bonnie interjected her opinion, and it was one I completely agreed with. "And besides, didn't he just drag you into the police station kicking and screaming like a child? What in the heavens would make you think he'd want to date you after that scene?"

Heather shot Bonnie a look that had no respect in it whatsoever. She feigned innocence when she smiled at Belle, flinched and pressed her hand into her chest. "Heavens, wherever do you think I'm going? I simply asked a question."

"Em hmm," Belle said. "Considering your multi-year conniption fit and inability to move on from the disillusion of your relationship with Austin Emmerson, one would think you'd be a little more sensitive to Lily's situation."

Heather blinked. "And what situation is that exactly? Who broke up with whom?"

"Oh, this is getting good," Bonnie said. "I don't need to watch me no reality TV tonight. We got better stuff right here in Bramblett County."

I'd had enough. "Ladies, stop. We're here to learn about organizing and staging our homes for their best financial resale, not to get pithy with each other and fight about boys. You'd think we'd be past that stage by now. And besides, a friend just died." I narrowed my eyes at Heather. "Whether you can admit it or not, Savannah was your friend once, and now she's dead. Have some respect for that friendship."

Heather's eyes shifted toward the floor. Bonnie and Henrietta mumbled. I pointed at them. "Ladies, with all due respect, hush."

Their eyes widened, but their mouths stayed shut.

Caroline barely moved, and without even looking at her, I knew Belle was about ready to do her happy dance.

"Okay then, let's get started with today's class." I flipped on my computer and opened my Powerpoint presentation. "Since we didn't get to finish the tour yesterday, I'll go ahead and review the points and add the details we would have seen in Savannah's house as we discuss them. If you have questions, feel free to ask, but please, keep them on point. Given the terrible tragedy, I'm not going to discuss the Armstrong home in particular, but staging and decluttering concepts in general."

The first slide explained that home owners must view their homes from the perspective of a buyer, not a seller. "We have to take an honest look at our homes to determine the purpose and value of each room. We must see past the memories, the photos, the things we've added throughout the years and distinguish the good from the bad."

The women nodded.

"And to do that, we must be truly objective. Once we determine the value of each room, decide on its purpose, we must remove everything that doesn't suit that purpose, and most everything that personalizes it to us. Buyers want to imagine themselves in the home. They want to see themselves sitting in the chair by the fireplace. They don't want to imagine you there, staring at a picture of your great uncle."

"No one wants to stare at a picture of my great uncle. He fell out the ugly tree and done hit every branch on the way down," Bonnie said.

The rest of us laughed, except for Caroline who remained quiet, but it definitely broke the tension in the room.

Class went well after that, and we finished up without another mention of Savannah or Dylan. I assigned them homework—to which Bonnie and Henrietta hemmed and hawed, but I explained it was for their own good because I might just go ahead and give grades after all, so they decided to go ahead and do it.

I asked Caroline to wait to leave. Heather's dislike of my whispering to Caroline was obvious from the snarl she directed my way. Belle caught on and distracted Heather by walking her to her car.

"Are you okay?" I asked Caroline.

"Yes."

Upon closer observation, I noticed her eyes were a touch glossy.

"Are you…" I wasn't sure how to ask what I needed to ask, so I just blurted it out. "Stoned?"

Someone coughed, and I turned around to see Ellie Jean in the room. She shrugged and scooted out.

Caroline half-smiled. "Oh heavens, no. William's mother gave me one of her relaxation pills because I'm a little tense is all." She picked up her bag and then dropped it on the ground. "Whoospie."

"Caroline, did you drive here?"

"Goodness gracious, no. My William dropped me off." She giggled. "I'm in no condition to drive."

I had a feeling the confrontation with Savannah, her subsequent murder and Caroline's questioning at the sheriff's office was a bit much for her, and that's why she'd taken whatever it was William's mother had given her. "When is William coming to get you?"

"When class is over." She wobbled a little as she stood. "He'll be outside."

"Okay. How about I take you out there?" I grabbed her bag. "Let me get this for you."

"Well, all right then, if you insist." She walked like someone who was being asked to walk a straight line for a drunk driving test. Focused on her feet, her eyes locked on their every move, but she was unable to keep steady.

William headed into the library as we exited the main doors. He rushed to her side, and she fell into him.

"Oh, William dear, I'm so sleepy."

"What did she take?" I asked.

"My mother gave her a Xanax. She didn't sleep at all last night, and this morning she was so anxious and stressed out about everything, I didn't know what to do. I called my mom, and she rushed over, told Caroline to take the pill and go to bed. Caroline took the pill but insisted on coming to class. Said it would look bad if she didn't. I didn't want her to, but I'm not the boss of her, you know?"

I nodded. "When a woman makes up her mind, no one's the boss of her."

"Ain't that the truth." He secured his hold on his wife and smiled at me. "Thanks for getting her out here."

"No problem. Let me know how she's doing okay?"

"I will. She's having a rough time of it. Savannah's death really threw her for a loop."

"That and her coming back to town in general."

He blinked. "I guess so." He stood with his wife leaning against him. "Well, thanks again." He propped her up to walk and headed to his car.

~

Belle and I stayed at the library to prepare for the next class and handle some work related items. She wanted to discuss Dylan, but I refused. "I can't talk about him now."

"Are you sure?"

I nodded. "I just need some distance from it all right now."

"Got it. Can we talk about Savannah?"

I shoved some papers into a file. "Yes, let's do that."

"But it's going to include Dylan."

"I know, but that's different."

"I saw him this morning. I made my statement."

I didn't know she'd gone there, too. "Really? I was there this morning. When were you there?"

"I didn't go to the station. I met him early, at Millie's. I gave it there."

My stomach lurched. Dylan met with Belle in a casual environment and with me in an official one. I guess I deserved that.

"He told me Savannah died from strangulation. That's horrible."

I swallowed a lump building in the back of my throat. "I know. I can't even imagine."

"I read about it. It's quick, so there's that."

"I guess, but still, it's an awful way to die."

"Definitely. Did he tell you he's planning on arresting someone?" she asked.

"Did he tell you that?"

"Oh, no. He wouldn't even tell me who his suspects are,

though it's pretty obvious. Told me to leave it alone. I just thought maybe he said something to you, you know, seeing as…" She let that comment lie there, unfinished.

"He told me to stay out of it, too, remember? And he reiterated that this morning. But, I have my own list of suspects, and I'm pretty sure he's got the same ones."

"Well, I think he needs to arrest Austin Emmerson. Obviously, he did it."

"Why do you think that?"

"Savannah was strangled. You've got to be pretty strong to do that. Plus, he had on that red hoodie jacket, and she was divorcing him." She leaned back in her chair. "I've always kind of thought he was a snake in the grass anyway, especially after what he did to Heather."

It takes two to tango, you know."

"Oh, honey, I know, but still. I just can't see a woman killing someone with her bare hands."

I wasn't so sure about that. Love and money made people do crazy things. "I don't know. Something doesn't feel right about it all to me, and remember, Heather's red hoodie was in the Armstrong's house."

"You're going to do it, aren't you?"

"Do what?" I asked.

"Exactly what Dylan told you not to, get involved in his investigation."

"I'm not going to get involved. I'm just going to do a little research of my own. I feel a little responsible for this, and I think I owe it to Savannah."

Belle sighed. "You weren't the one that set her up in the class. That was all me."

"It's not your fault. The class was my idea, and Savannah didn't have to show her parent's home. She did that with intent. It was my fault for not stopping her from doing that. I shouldn't have let it get as far as it did. I put her in harm's way."

"We both did, Lily."

"I could have said no to her, but I didn't, and I need to make it right."

"Me, too."

"No, Belle. This is on my shoulders, not yours. Besides, your relationship with Matthew is new. You don't need to mess it up by getting involved in a murder investigation."

"Oh, so you can mess up your relationship, but I can't?"

"Yes." I nodded my head in a short, quick rhythm. "That's exactly what I'm saying."

"My boyfriend is only the deputy sheriff, so don't you think it would be less of a problem if I did something?"

I furrowed my brow. "Honey, that is all kinds of crazy, but either way, no. I need you to hold down the fort here. Okay?"

She stuck her chin high in the air and made some strange huffy sound by blowing air out of her nose. "Fine. It doesn't matter anyway. I know you'll keep me in the loop."

"Of course, I will. You're my best friend."

We finished the items on our mutual to do list, and Belle left for a prospective listing appointment. I needed to follow up on our current client listings, check on the progress of the condos being built on Myrtle Redbecker's old property and pick Bo up at doggy daycare. We had some training to practice before puppy school later.

The busy work distracted my heart and allowed me to forget about Dylan. I didn't forget about Savannah though. In fact, I couldn't stop thinking about her and who might have killed her.

The condo unit construction was progressing fine. They had a real estate company coming in to do the actual unit sales, but I'd worked out an arrangement for a pre-construction commitment commission as well as a higher split rate for anyone we brought to the table who purchased a unit, so it was important for me to keep tabs on the quality of their work. I'd already got contracts on four units and expected one more in the near future. A new lacrosse coach had been hired at the high school, and he'd fallen in love with one of the models. The first building was scheduled for completion in two months, with a ready move in date a month later, and I hoped that stayed on track. I'd sold one of those to the coach, and he'd been paying a ridiculously high rent for a one bedroom house in town while waiting. Teacher's salaries weren't accommodating to high rent prices, especially in counties with limited rentals.

I left the condo property and bumped into Austin Emmerson on my way to pick up Bo. Literally bumped into him inside the gas station. "Oh, hey." I wasn't exactly sure what to say to him.

He bounced on the tips of his toes and rubbed the spot that connected his left shoulder to his neck. "Hey, I was planning on coming to see you later. You got a minute now?"

I tapped my electronic pedometer to check the time. "Just a quick one. What's up?" I wanted to talk to him also, but I'd hope it would be in a more private setting.

He pulled me to the side. "Can we talk outside or maybe go for a beer or something?"

"I don't have time for a beer." I didn't drink anyway, but it wasn't something I usually discussed. "But let me pay for my things, and I'll meet you outside. I have to get my dog at day care and go to puppy class."

He pushed his eyebrows together. "Your dog's at daycare?"

"It's a pretty popular trend now. I'm surprised you've never heard of it." I walked toward the checkout counter. "Give me a second."

He paced the front sidewalk of the gas station convenience store while I paid for my things. I hadn't seen Austin in years but he wasn't the same guy I knew in college. His shoulders slumped and his chest kind of caved in. Insecurity and depression replaced the elitist southern charm and overbearing confidence that had always annoyed me in college.

"What's up?" I asked.

We walked to my car.

"Your boyfriend told me not to leave town. He thinks I killed my wife."

I didn't tell him Dylan wasn't my boyfriend. "Did you?"

His eyes widened. "What? No. I...why would I do that? I loved her."

"She was divorcing you. She said you'd cheated on her, and she was tired of it."

"I never cheated on Savannah."

"Just because you paid for it doesn't mean it's not cheating."

"Uh. I...I don't have to pay for sex."

"Savannah said something different."

"She's lying. Was lying. That's not why we were getting divorced. She left me because of the money." He shook his hands at the side of his head. "She had an argument with my parents and...and they cut us off." He tugged on his shirt. "Look at me. Do I look like you remember?" He held up his left foot. "These are Berluti shoes. They cost over twenty-one hundred bucks, and they've got mud on them. Do you think I'd let that happen if I didn't have to?"

He was disheveled and wearing the same clothes he had on the day we discovered Savannah's body, including the red hoodie. That wasn't like Austin. He grew up in in a big house in one of the wealthiest communities in Atlanta. Buckhead people didn't wear dirty clothes, and they certainly didn't wear the same clothes more than once a week.

"She did say she told your parents you two should manage your own money. She said you were getting an allowance, and she was tired of it."

"Not an allowance. A trust. I received a monthly payment from my trust, and they stopped that because of the things she said to them and because she was over-spending every month. She kept going to them for cash and they refused to give her any more, so she left." He rubbed his eyes and dragged his hand down his face. "I have a couple hundred bucks to my name and that's it." He leaned against my car. "I don't know what I'm going to do. This is bad."

"You're not winning friends here, Austin."

He looked me straight in the eyes. "I didn't kill her, Lily. You've got to believe me. I wanted to work things out. I don't care about the money. I didn't care about the money. I told my parents that. I told Savannah that, and that's why she left. She said the only reason she married me was for the money. Said she never loved me and would have chosen that loser Billy if she'd wanted to marry for love."

Billy? What was he—oh no, Billy. Back in college everyone called William Abernathy Billy. "You mean Caroline's husband?"

"Yes, Billy. They were together for over a year, but no one knew about it. Savannah said she loved him, but she didn't want to stay in Bramblett County. She didn't want to live on a corn maze. She thought she was better than that."

I leaned on my car, too. "So, it's true. Savannah and William really were together. Poor Caroline."

"I didn't kill my wife. I loved her. I still love her." He cried, and I watched as the tears fell from his eyes. "You've got to talk to your boyfriend, Lily. Please."

He was right. I did have to talk to Dylan, at least about Savannah and William, and definitely before Caroline found out. "I don't know what I can do, but I'll try to say something."

"So, you believe me?"

I did believe him. That meant if Austin didn't kill Savannah, I had only two possible suspects, Heather and Caroline, and since I'd just found out that William did cheat on his wife, Caroline's threats looked worse than before.

CHAPTER 5

*B*o and his drooling jowls earned him the most popular puppy award in doggy day care. Well, that and the fact that he snuggled onto every lap he could, every chance he got. He was definitely a ladies' pup. I should have been offended, but I'd learned a lap was a lap and no longer took it personally.

There was just enough time to feed the big lug–and myself— and walk to the park for puppy training, so that's what we did. The walk was quick, except for a few marking stops and over-whelming stiff scrutinization of a leaf, rock and interesting spot on the ground. Class also flew by, probably because only two other puppies showed up, so we finished in almost half the time.

I knew if we went straight home I'd end up either on the couch or the back patio fretting about Dylan or obsessing about Savannah's murder, neither of which were fair to Bo, so even though he was tired, he rallied, and we took the scenic route home, extending the walk another fifteen minutes.

I loved the scenic route because it took us by the abandoned barn I used to sneak into as a kid. Most of it was gone now, the wood that hadn't rotted either stolen by people or destroyed by kudzu, leaving only the frame of the old building standing.

Most of Georgia believed whomever introduced kudzu to America did so with the sole intention of destroying the South. The weed grew like a middle school boy in puberty. Nothing stopped it except a strong, deep fire, and often that wasn't enough. Some landscape professionals said serious weed killers took it out, but if the vine showed up on a residential lawn, using something strong like that would kill everything else before it even touched the nasty vine.

Kudzu migrated from the Northeast to Georgia as a grass replacement. Georgia clay, our nearly impossible to penetrate, hard, orange dirt, didn't allow much to take root, and kudzu was the perfect ground cover. Until it wasn't. Back when it first took over the state, or at least started to, and people went missing, it was assumed they were eaten by the weedy vine. People would say things like, "Old Johnny boy, he was a good fellow. Too bad he took to dyin' out in that there kudzu. Walked out in it one night an ain't never come back."

Every time I saw the weedy vine intertwining itself around some poor, dying tree or old building, I shivered. My father used to tell me never get too close to it and most definitely never touch it, or it would eat me alive. At fifteen Belle and I touched it to see what would happen, and of course, she made me touch it first. Given that neither of us went missing, I suspected most people that had either wanted to, or did because of something other than the kudzu. Neither of those options made the old tale fun though.

Bo rushed to the brush of weed and piddled on it. I imagined that was his own version of rebellion toward the useless ground cover and rubbed his ears. "Good boy. If anything can kill that destructive vine, it's your urine, big boy."

We spent the rest of the walk enjoying the cool evening breeze and listening to the night sounds. Bo jumped and yelped in fear at the frog that hopped out in front of him, and I laughed hysterically and then felt bad when he hid behind my legs. "It's just a little toad, buddy. It's not going to hurt you."

The poor frog was probably more scared of him. We watched him hop into the grass and make his little sounds to warn all his friends to stay clear of the monsters on the sidewalk.

When we got home there was an envelope taped onto my front door. I assumed it was from Dylan and tossed it on the kitchen table without opening it. An hour later, after getting ready for bed, I poured myself a glass of iced water and stared at the envelope. It just sat on the table, mocking me and begging me to open it.

I knew what it said. Something similar to, sorry, I didn't mean to upset you. Please forgive me. Blah, blah, blah. I didn't want to read it. I wasn't ready to read it, but some part of me, the compulsive part, apparently, wanted to read it, and my hand snatched up the envelope, ripped it open and pulled out the letter.

It wasn't from Dylan. In fact, it wasn't signed at all, but I knew who it was from the minute I read the single typed line.

If you know what's good for you, you'll do what your boyfriend says.

I eyed the typed note. At first my heart beat increased, and I went into panic mode, but that subsided quickly, and then I got angry. The anger diminished just as fast, and then I just didn't care.

"Really," I said to my dog. "This, again?" I waved the note at him, and he jumped for it. I pitched the note back onto the table, filled his water and got him a treat.

How many times would I be threatened by people involved in murders in Bramblett County?

While Bo munched on his big milk bone, I made a security check through the house, checking every door and window. I grabbed the note from the table again and sat on the couch with my cell phone. I flipped the phone in my hand over and over, postponing the inevitable. I knew what I had to do. I just didn't want to do it. I refused to make the call. Instead, I snapped a photo of the note and texted it to Dylan.

He responded in under a minute with, "I'll be there in five."

And he was.

~

Dylan pulled on the window over the kitchen sink.

"I already checked that."

He pinched his lips together and marched into my family room, where he yanked on the windows there, too.

I stood in the doorway with my arms crossed over my chest. "Checked those, also. And the one in the bedrooms, bathrooms, and my office. They're all locked. So is the front door and the door to the patio."

He half smiled and then reached out his hand. "May I see the note, please?"

I handed it to him.

He unfolded the note and read it, then he glared at me. "I told you to stay out of it."

I returned his scowl. "I haven't done anything."

He tossed the note on the table behind my couch. "Well, the killer thinks you have, and now you're in danger. I knew this would happen. I knew it."

"I'm in danger because it's the third body in just about as many months that I've either found or been a part of finding. That's why the killer thinks I'm involved."

He contemplated that for a second. "The point is, you're not safe. You're going to need protection."

"I've got Bo."

Dylan sized up the monster-sized puppy chasing his tail in the corner of the room and laughed. "Bo is a great dog, but he's not protection."

I stepped to the side to block his view. "He is, too."

"I'll get a deputy to keep an eye on your tomorrow, but for tonight, I'm staying with you."

My eyes lifted to his. "You don't—no. You can't do that. We broke up. That's not appropriate."

"I didn't realize we'd officially broken up, but I stayed here before when we weren't dating, so what's the difference now?"

I stuffed my hands into my pockets. "It's just different, Dylan. I can stay at Belle's."

"With Bo?" He laughed again. "You really think that's a good idea?"

I glanced over at my pup who'd stopped chasing his tail to chew on the corner of my brick fireplace instead. "She's had him there before."

"Is that good for his teeth?"

I doubted it, but I had a feeling the fireplace would suffer more damage. "Bo, no."

Bo's big puppy eyes drooped, and he whined like I'd just ruined his life.

"That's not good for you."

"I'll sleep on the couch if for no other reason than to make sure your big lug of a mutt here doesn't chip a tooth on a brick."

"He sleeps with me, so you don't have to worry about that." I didn't argue. Arguing with Dylan was like arguing with my mom when she'd made a decision about something. It just wasn't worth it. Besides, even though I would never admit it to him, I felt safe knowing he was there with me.

The couch was easier access to whatever might happen, he said, and I agreed. I set up the sheets and blankets for him, and we sat and talked about the case—sort of—over iced tea, before going to bed. It was civil and almost normal.

"I ran into Austin Emmerson at the gas station."

"Let me guess, he told you he didn't kill his wife."

"Yes."

"And you believe him."

"Yes."

He leaned his head back on my couch. "Lily, you know that's what every guilty person says, right?"

I nodded. "This is different though."

He rolled his eyes. "Come on, that's what he wants you to think. What sob story did he tell you? Wait. Let me guess. He loved her. He would have done anything for her. That kind of thing?"

If I wasn't a proper southern lady, I would have tossed my iced tea on him. Okay, so I also didn't want to ruin my couch, but also, I was a proper southern lady. "He said Savannah only married him for his money."

"Well, I can see that."

"I know, and she did say she left him because he couldn't man up to his parents about their finances, that she was tired of having to go to them for money all the time because he spent it all on..." I hesitated, trying to find an appropriate way to phrase it. "On paid pleasure."

He shifted his head toward me, and I blushed. "You mean he paid for sex?"

My face heated up like an oven.

He smiled. "You're cute when you're embarrassed."

I smiled without intending to. "Stop it, you know I hate talking about that stuff."

He placed his hand on my knee and squeezed. "Yes, I know. It's adorable."

I wanted to either melt or crawl into a hole and hide. I couldn't decide which. "Seriously though, he said he never did that, that she was the one that spent all their money, and when she went to his parents for more, I guess they'd had enough and just stopped giving it to them all together, so she left."

"When the money tree died, she hit the road?"

"According to him. He said she told him she'd married him

for his money, and that if she'd wanted to marry for love, she would have married Billy."

"Billy?" He sat up. "You mean William Abernathy?"

I nodded. "Apparently the rumor is true. Austin said William and Savannah were together over a year."

"And nobody knew?"

"Everyone suspected something, but no one knew for sure."

"If they were in love, why didn't he just break up with Caroline for Savannah?"

"Austin didn't say William loved Savannah. He said she loved him."

"Interesting."

"I know. It adds a whole additional layer to this, don't you think? Now Caroline looks more serious in the suspect department."

He drained the last of his iced tea, made a slight gulping sound as he swallowed it down and set the glass on the coaster on my coffee table. "Actually, it looks a lot worse for William than it does for Caroline."

"Why is that?"

"Because I saw William earlier today, and you know what he was wearing?"

"A red hoodie."

"Bingo."

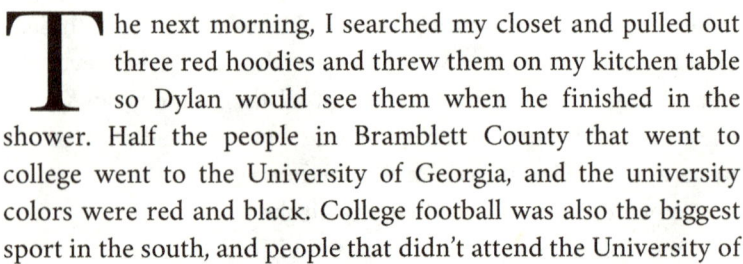

The next morning, I searched my closet and pulled out three red hoodies and threw them on my kitchen table so Dylan would see them when he finished in the shower. Half the people in Bramblett County that went to college went to the University of Georgia, and the university colors were red and black. College football was also the biggest sport in the south, and people that didn't attend the University of

Georgia were also big supporters, so given those two factors alone, one had to assume that more than three quarters of the county owned a red jacket or hoodie of some sort. That, I intended to prove to Dylan, couldn't be the primary piece of evidence when considering someone a suspect.

I handed Dylan a hot cup of coffee. He took a sip, saw the hoodies and held one in his hand. "They're nice, but I don't think they're my size."

"That's not the point."

"I know the point, and I'm not saying that's the only reason to consider William."

"Then what are the other reasons?"

"If Savannah and William did have a relationship, and William had kept it secret all this time, then all of a sudden, Savannah's back in town, it's possible William got scared. Maybe he thought she would tell Caroline the truth? Maybe she threatened to, and he felt he had to stop her? Who knows. My point is, there's more to this situation than either of us know, and it's my job to figure it out."

I nodded. "I understand."

"And I need you to do me a favor, okay?"

"I'll try."

"I need you to keep the note you received private. I don't want it making the rounds around town, okay?"

"Okay." I conceded to the right decision. "You were right, by the way. I'm glad you stayed here last night. It did make me feel better. Thank you."

He stepped toward me and surprisingly, I didn't back away, even when he kissed my forehead. "I don't want anything to happen to you, Little Bean. I'm staying here tonight, too."

"Really, it's okay. I can stay at Belle's."

"You can't tonight. She's going to Atlanta with Matt, so you're stuck with me for at least one more night."

He offered to take Bo to doggy daycare, and I accepted the

offer. I needed to pick up the class breakfast items and coffee from Millie's, and Dylan helping just made things easier for me.

He offered to drive me to Millie's, but I wanted to walk instead. Nearly obsessed with gaining steps on my electronic pedometer, I didn't want to miss the opportunity to make my seventeen thousand steps a day goal. I hadn't gone to a spin class in over two weeks and hitting that step goal was the next best thing.

I took the short cut to Millie's and walked past the side road that led to the deserted barn again. It was rush hour, and even though Bramblett County was small, we still had a fair amount of traffic, enough to make me have to wait and use the cross walk to cross. Ahead of me was a woman with long red hair and a man that looked a lot like William. When they turned toward each other, I noticed the scruffy beard and short brown hair of the man, and I knew right then it was definitely him.

I stopped and tried to hide behind the light post, even though the thing was half my size. They hadn't noticed me, but not because I was a stellar private investigator, because they were too involved with each other at that moment to pay attention.

I wouldn't describe their moment as intimate, but I couldn't say it was platonic either. There was something going on, I just didn't know what. Caroline and I may not have stayed all that close over the years, but I still considered her a friend, more so than Heather must have, and I wasn't going to let the two of them do whatever it was they were doing, not in front of me anyway.

I gathered my nerve and pushed forward and away from the security of the light post and walked toward them. When they finally did see me, I was only a few feet away. "Hey y'all." I waved my hand high over my head and smiled so big my face hurt. "Whatcha doin' out here together so early in the morning?" I laid on the sweet southern girl charm so thick you could taste the sugar oozing from me all the way on the south side of Hartsfield Jackson Airport.

Heather flipped her hair and combed her fingers gently through it. "Oh, hey."

William nodded and then stuffed his hands in his pockets. He did not look pleased.

"Now Billy," I used his college name on purpose. "What's wrong? Did Chevy stop making trucks or something?" I winked. "You're not going to have to go and buy yourself a Ford now, are you?"

"You're funny, Lilybit." He nodded at Heather. "We'll catch up later. I got to run."

She smiled. "Okay, see you soon."

"Well, he's as happy as a pig in mud, isn't he?"

Heather scowled.

"Oh my. I see someone peed in your cornflakes this morning, didn't they?"

She pressed her lips together. "Why are you always so happy? Are you faking it or is that just how you are?"

I ignored the comment and crooked my finger for her to follow. "I need to get the scones for class. Come on. I'll buy you a latte."

She huffed but followed.

We picked up the order, and she sipped the latte on the short walk to the library.

"So, why don't you tell me what's going on with you and William?"

She avoided making eye contact. "There's nothing going on with me and William. Why would you say something like that?"

"Come on Heather. I wasn't born yesterday. I saw you two at the bridge, and things looked pretty comfy a little bit ago between you guys, so let's be real here, okay?"

She stopped next to the library entrance and a row of garbage cans and in a condescending tone, said, "Bless your heart. You think just because you had a little fling with the county sheriff and you were involved in that old biddy's murder you have the right to go sticking your nose into everyone else's business?"

"I never said that."

"Oh honey, you don't have to. You wear it on your sleeve. I mean, just look at yourself, all prim and proper and not one single hair out of place. Who do you think you are, Nancy Drew?" She sipped her drink, the one I purchased. "Let me tell you something, Lily Sprayberry. If you're not careful, that little nose of yours might just get you in some serious trouble. The kind you might not be able to get out of. You understand?" She dropped the cup into one of the garbage cans. "I don't think I'll finish your little class after all. I only joined because I felt sorry for you anyway."

CHAPTER 6

"She what? How dare her." Belle's nostrils flared.

"I know."

"Well, if she thinks she's getting a refund, she's got another thing coming."

Ellie Jean stepped up to the side of the front desk and coughed. "Are you two all right?"

I straightened my blouse. "Oh, yes, ma'am. We're fine."

"Right as rain, Ms. Pruitt," Belle smiled.

"Do you need help with all that?"

Belle had a box of things from the office, and I had my usual bag and the goodies from Millie's. "You know what, that would be wonderful." I placed Millie's bags on the counter. "Would you mind helping with those? If you haven't eaten yet, you're welcome to a scone or two and some coffee from the tumbler. "We'll definitely have extra today."

"And the rest of the week," Belle interjected.

"Oh? Why is that?"

"Heather isn't going to be participating any longer."

Ellie Jean nodded. "Well, God bless her, she's missing out on a world of knowledge then, isn't she?"

Belle smiled. "Yes, ma'am. She is, and thank you for saying that."

Ellie Jean returned the smile. "I always liked you two. You were always kind to me and my daughter, Faith. Now the others, they weren't so. Why, my poor Faith used to come home crying from the things those girls would do to her."

Faith didn't run in our social circle, but I'd always liked her. She was a little on the shy side, and she'd been a great cheerleader, making the football squad but never quite passing the final try outs for the competition squad, though that wasn't because she wasn't good enough. Savannah's parents donated the printing services for the school's extracurricular activities, and the principal made it a point of making sure Savannah got what she wanted when she wanted it. It wasn't fair, but printing wasn't cheap, and the principal had a budget.

"I know Savannah wasn't all that nice to her, but I really liked your daughter."

"I liked her, too," Belle said.

"And I know she liked both of you." She carried the bag of scones into the conference room. "I would love a cup of that coffee. The coffee here tastes like liquid tar."

Belle grimaced. "Ew."

"I think they buy it on purpose. Keeps people from staying here too long."

"But I thought you'd want to have people hang out in the library?" I asked.

"Oh, I do, of course. It's the board that doesn't. They want them to check out the books and leave." She leaned in toward us. "And I'll tell you a secret. They don't even want them to return them on time anymore. They make a pretty penny on the late fees, let me tell you." She nodded. "Why, I could buy myself a fancy car with those late fees if they went to my pocketbook."

Belle pressed her hand to her chest. "Heavens, I think I might have an overdue book from high school. I can't even imagine what the fees are on that thing."

Ellie Jean winked at her. "Don't you worry that pretty little head of yours. I have a feeling those late fees won't matter much longer."

She let out a heavy sigh. "Oh, thank you Ms. Pruitt. You just relieved a world of stress for me."

I poured Ellie Jean a cup of coffee and handed it to her. "Thank you so much for helping. I appreciate it."

"You're welcome dear. If you need anything else, why, you just come get me, okay?"

"Yes, ma'am."

She scooted out just as Henrietta and Bonnie came rushing in.

"Did you hear the news?" Bonnie asked.

"Oh, you've just got to cancel class today. We can't miss the excitement down at the station," Henrietta said.

"What news? What excitement?" Belle asked.

"Why, I can't believe you two don't know, what with the fact that you're both dating our men in blue and all," Bonnie said.

"Bonnie, for Heaven's sake, they wear brown, not blue. You need to get your eyes checked."

Bonnie swatted her friend's arm. "I know that. It's an expression."

"Well, it's a dumb expression, and it makes you sound dumb, too."

Bonnie's back stiffened. "A lot of things you say make you sound dumb, but I don't say nothing to you about it, and don't call me dumb."

"Dumb, dumb, dumb."

Bonnie snarled at her friend.

"Ladies, can you please tell us what's going on?"

Henrietta plucked a scone from the bag and talked after she

bit into it. "Rumor has it your man has gone and arrested him a suspect in that floozy's murder. The rich husband from the city."

Bonnie had poured herself a cup of coffee and held it in her hand with her little pinky sticking out. "I don't think he did it. You might could tell him that too, next time you see him."

"He's arrested Austin Emmerson?"

Henrietta nodded. "He sure has, and contrary to what this old bat says, I think he's got the killer. It's always the spouse. Don't any of you watch crime TV shows?"

Belle pointed at me. "She does."

I nudged her shoulder with mine. "Where did you hear this?" Dylan hadn't mentioned anything to me earlier.

"Old Man Goodson just told us. Said Billy Ray stopped him on his way to the station and told him," Bonnie said.

That didn't make sense. Just a while ago he'd told me he considered William Abernathy and possibly even Caroline suspects, so why would he go ahead and arrest Austin? He must have found additional evidence. Evidence he hadn't told me about.

"Did he happen to say why Dylan decided to arrest Austin Emmerson?"

"Because he did it," Henrietta said. "What other reason does he need?"

I squeezed my hands into fists. "No, that's not what I mean. I mean did he say if the sheriff's office found new evidence or something?"

"Oh, that. Well, yes, I guess they got something back from some lab or something and said it matched him." She glanced at Bonnie. "I can't remember what it was. Something about dust in the house maybe?"

Bonnie nodded. "I don't get it, though. We was there with y'all, and that house could have passed my meemaw's white glove test. There wasn't no sprinkle of dust nowhere."

Belle angled her head at me. "Dust?"

"Yeah, that's what we did when Old Man Goodson said it to us. Said they dusted the house and found evidence that it was the husband."

I finally made the connection, thanks to Old Man Goodson. "Oh, you mean they dusted the house for fingerprints and found Austin's?"

They both nodded at the same time. "Yeah, that's it," Bonnie said. "Why'd they put dust in the house though? Sounds crazy to me."

Belle suppressed a giggle, and I briefly explained the process.

That time Henrietta whacked her friend on the arm. "I done told you they was talking about another kind of dust, you old fool."

Bonnie rubbed her arm but ignored her friend. "Anyway, the whole town's gathering at the sheriff's office. We're bringing sandwiches from Millie's."

"You might could bring the scones," Henrietta said.

"And that tumbler of coffee since you won't be needin' it here," Bonnie added.

Belle and I glanced at each other. She grabbed the scones, and I grabbed the coffee tumbler. "Can you drive? I walked here."

She nodded and asked the ladies if they needed a ride.

Bonnie smiled and wiggled a little in place. "Nope. Old Man Goodson's picking us up."

Henrietta wiggled, too. "We got ourselves a double date."

Belle whispered in my ear. "Isn't Old Man Goodson married?"

"I thought so," I whispered back.

Henrietta narrowed her eyes at us. "You think I'm like that friend of yours? You should be ashamed of yourself. I'm no floozy." She pulled a hanky from her purse and dabbed at her eyes. "Bonnie, let's go. I don't need these hussies disrespecting me." She wrapped her purse strap over her arm and flipped around to leave.

"Henrietta, wait, please." I rushed toward her. "That's not at all what we meant. I'm sorry." I chose my words carefully. "It's just that the last time I spoke to Mr. Goodson in detail, I had the impression he was married."

Bonnie jumped to her friend's defense. "His wife's been sleeping in the guest room for two years now. Filed for divorce months ago, but she don't want to leave the house. Says it's hers, and she's staying in it. Don't care what he does with his life. He can stay or go, but the house is hers."

Belle's eyes caught mine, and we shared the kind of look only best friends understood. The kind that says, oh crap, we messed up. Her eyes said it was my job to fix it. Her eyes always said that because that was my thing, and I did a better job at being polite and kind.

"Oh, I'm sorry for Mr. Goodson. I can only imagine how hard that must be, but I'm glad he's got Henrietta to share some happiness with. I'm sure you brighten his day, and I'm so sorry if we offended you. Please, I hope you know we didn't intend to do that. We would never do that intentionally."

A smile stretched across Henrietta's face, and her eyes softened. She stuffed the hanky back into her purse. "Well, I might could see how you'd think otherwise. Most of town knows, but you're part of the younger crowd, so it might could have skipped right on by you."

Belle nodded. "It might have. I'm sorry, too, Henrietta. You two certainly deserve to be happy, but may I ask a question?"

Henrietta nodded, though slowly, and I knew she was hesitant to agree.

Belle smiled and pointed to Bonnie. "Old man Gib—I mean, Mr. Gibson is a nice man, but you two ladies are quite the whippersnappers, and a whole lot of women for one man." She winked at them both. "How is that poor man still alive?"

They both giggled, and for the first time they didn't need the pink liquid rouge they'd smeared on their faces that morning. It was absolutely adorable and made me giggle, too.

Once Bonnie could speak, she said, "Oh, sweetie, that man couldn't handle the two of us if he was twins. He's gone back to get Billy Ray for me."

We all laughed again.

"Well look at you two," Belle said. "When we grow up, we definitely want to be like you ladies."

"Sweetie, everyone wants to be like us," Henrietta said.

I pointed at them both and then at my eyes. "You ladies better behave. I'm watching you."

"We've done all the behaving required of us. It's time to have some fun," Henrietta said.

They both giggled and rushed out of the room.

"We are so going to be them when we're old," Belle said, and followed them out of the room.

I trailed behind her, secretly hoping that, at their age, I wasn't wrapped up in the dating world in any way whatsoever.

Belle stopped me on our way out. "Hey, what about Caroline? Should we tell her class is canceled?"

"I'll send her a text."

~

Belle questioned the arrest as she drove. "Austin's fingerprints would be all over Savannah's parent's house, don't you think?"

"Yes, and no. Yes, definitely, at least before we did the decluttering, cleaning and staging, but I'm not sure about after."

"Is that enough reason to arrest him for murder though?"

"I don't know. Why don't you ask your boyfriend?"

"Afraid to ask Dylan?"

"Not afraid, but he's probably a little busy at the moment. And honestly, I'm trying really hard not to mention the case. I'd prefer he bring it up first." That was my way of avoiding asking him. It kind of upset me that he hadn't mentioned any of the fingerprint issue to me the night before, and while I understood his motive, I still couldn't help but be annoyed.

"How's that working out for you?"

"Not that great, really."

"How about this? My phone is in my purse. Would you text Matthew for me?"

"Great idea." I tapped out a quick text asking the question and mentioned that we were headed that way.

He responded. "Keep this between us please, but the prints were primarily on the front door and the trunk. Found a few on her clothes but that wouldn't be unusual."

I replied. "Since Lily and Savannah had just done a major cleaning, would that have eliminated a lot of the previous fingerprints?"

"Technology can uncover latent prints regular cleaning products can't remove."

"So, couldn't those prints have been from months ago?"

"On the door, yes, but the Armstrong's just bought that trunk two months ago. When we spoke to Austin the day of Savannah's murder, he said he hadn't been there on or before that night but apparently, he had."

I'd read the texts out loud as Matthew responded. That last one made both Belle and I cringe.

"Oh, crap," she said.

"My thoughts exactly. He must have lied to me." I filled her in on my discussion with him.

"Oh no, so Savannah and William did have a fling?"

"Well, I don't know now. I don't know what to believe anymore."

She pulled into the parking lot of the sheriff's office alongside the rest of the county. Packed full of cars and pickup trucks, if I didn't know better, I'd have thought we were at opening night for a Marvel movie at the drive-in theater.

Old Man Goodson honked as he drove by in his old Chevy pickup truck with Henrietta and Bonnie hanging out the window waving at us.

Belle groaned. "We need a serious life makeover, don't we?"

"Honey, if you're comparing us to them, we'll lose every single time."

She parked her car on the grass in between the parking lot and the road in the last spot available, and we both hopped out, zigzagging our way through the crowd and up to the front where we could get the best view. Belle had no reservations about pushing through everyone, and I just held onto her hand and followed behind her. We landed right next to William and Caroline.

"Oh my gosh, can you believe it?" Caroline asked.

I glanced at William, who quickly looked away.

"Have you seen Heather?" I asked Caroline.

"Not today. I figured we weren't having class today what with this happening and all, so she probably did, too." She balanced on her husband's arm and bounced on her tiptoes, searching through the crowd. "Goodness, I can't see anything but a blur of heads a mile long, but I'm sure she's here somewhere."

"I doubt it," Belle said. "Hey, William, didn't you see her earlier today?"

I loved Belle so much.

He gave Belle a look filled with such disdain, I worried he might hurt her.

Belle ran with it, but instead of addressing him directly, used hit him where it hurt, or at least where it would most likely hurt later—his wife. "Goodness, what crawled up your husband's backside this morning? Did you two have a fight or something?"

She most assuredly had the face of an angel and the soul of a sinner.

Caroline's head shifted between Belle and William. "Why do you ask that?" She glanced back at her husband and brushed a hand over his cheek. "Darling, is something wrong? Did you see Heather this morning?"

He shook his head. "I just can't believe this is happening to an old friend, that's all."

I smiled at him, my resolve strengthening from Belle's bravery. "Yes, I'm sure that's it."

Caroline eyed her husband. "William dear, you didn't answer my question." Her tone was sticky-sweet, but her stiff posture and tilted head said she wasn't pleased.

He stepped toward her, enveloped her into his arms and kissed her. "I didn't? I thought I told you I ran into her on my way to Millie's to get your coffee. It was real quick. Said hi and that was about it. Saw Lily on the way, too."

"Yep, he sure did. We had ourselves a nice little chat, didn't we, old friend?"

He nodded. "That we did. Where'd the two of you wander off to after that?"

"Oh, I had to go to Millie's to get the coffee and things for the class, but I must have gotten there after you. Heather and I talked a bit first and went there together. She said she couldn't take the class anymore."

Caroline stuck out her bottom lip. "Oh no, that's too bad. I know she was wanting to move into one of the condos on the old Redbecker property. She said the class was helping her get ideas for how to decorate. Has herself a big client willing to pay her enough to afford the down payment on one of the one bedrooms there. She's really excited about it, too."

"Heather's buying one of the condos?" I asked.

Caroline nodded. "Can't believe she hasn't mentioned it to you. I told her she should talk with you about it. You might could get her a deal even."

"We definitely could get her a deal," Belle said. She tapped something into her phone. "I'm texting her about it now."

I grabbed her arm. "Maybe you should wait on that."

She clicked the button on the side of her iPhone. "Oh, yeah. Good idea."

In Belle's mind a deal was a deal, no matter what personal issues might be involved. Unfortunately, the real world didn't always work that way. If given the choice, I had a feeling Heather would choose to work with the builder's agent over us.

Just then Dylan walked onto the front steps of the sheriff's office with Matthew and another deputy by his side. Belle bounced on her tiptoes. "Oh, this is kind of exciting. Matthew's first big announcement with the county. Look how cute he looks." Her eyes sparkled. She hadn't said it, but it was obvious. Belle was in love.

I had to admit, Dylan looked mighty nice in his brown uniform and hat. All official-like and even a touch sexy. My stomach did a little flip, and I steadied myself to make it stop.

He held up his hands to quiet the crowd. "Everyone, please. I know we've all got better things to do, so I'll make this quick. Yes, we've arrested someone in the death of Savannah Emmerson. No, I'm not going to go into any details, but in Bramblett County, we all know word travels fast, so I'm confident y'all will make due on your own just fine."

The crowd let out a collective moan.

"He really is a cutie pie," Belle said.

"I know. It's horrible."

"Only because you were stupid enough to run and hide with your tail between your legs instead of owning your fears and dealing with them."

She knew me better than my own mother. "Hush."

"Emm hmm."

Dylan nodded to the crowd. "Now, now people. Come on, cut

us some slack. This is the way it's done. You want information, right?"

Several people in the crowd nodded, and I noticed Dylan's eyes locked with mine. "I'll get you the information but in due time. Just be patient. When I know you're safe, I'll let you know what I can. Okay?"

I nodded, because even though he was speaking to the crowd, I knew his words were meant for me.

He smiled. "Now go on, get out of here and get back to what you ought to be doing."

The crowd slowly dissipated. Other than a few reporters from the town paper and a straggler or two, no one really stuck around. Belle forced herself around the reporters to align herself next to Matthew. He tugged at one of her belt loops and drew her even closer. I stood in the background not wanting to bother Dylan or make any waves.

Dylan finished with the reporters and came toward me.

My frustration with him not telling me about the fingerprints got the best of me. "That was quick. Did you leave my place and go right to him?"

He shrugged. "This is a murder investigation, Lily. And not that it matters, but I had to wait for the final results from the dusting before doing anything."

Even though I understood his reasoning, I still didn't like it. "Do you really believe Austin killed her? Last night you led me to believe William and even Caroline could be suspects, too."

He removed his hat and rubbed his head. "Do you have some time to talk?"

"Class is canceled, so yes, a little." I followed him into the building and into his office.

He pulled a chair out on the front side of his desk. "Take a seat."

He crossed over to his side of the desk and sat down. "I know Matt told Belle some of the details. Has she filled you in?"

"Actually, that was me texting him because she was driving."

"Okay, then I'll go from there. I don't have to remind you that this is confidential, and that we—"

I held up my hand. "I got it."

He nodded and continued. "Mrs. Armstrong said trouble'd been brewing between Savannah and Austin for over six months. He hadn't tried to come there in that time, but if he had, neither she nor her husband would have allowed him inside."

"Ouch."

"According to her, Savannah made Austin out to be a monster, and Mr. and Mrs. Armstrong encouraged her to leave him. When she finally did, they asked her to come home and help with the house. It was their way of getting her out of that environment."

"He may have been a monster, but his parents are rich. They'll get him a big name attorney from Atlanta who'll poke all kinds of holes in your case. Do you really think those fingerprints are enough to cover reasonable doubt?"

He opened his drawer and pulled out a jump drive. "When our district attorney shows them this, yes." He popped the little drive into his laptop, pressed a few buttons and flipped the computer my direction.

A scene from what I thought was a very inappropriate movie I would never watch filled the screen, and I immediately threw my hands over my eyes. "Ew, no. Shut that off. I don't need to see —" I peeked through my fingers. "Oh, ick. That's Austin isn't it?" I pressed the balls of my palms into each eye. "Okay, you can turn it off now, really. I've seen enough."

He flipped the lid of his laptop.

"Validates what Savannah told you and what she told her parents. It also discredits Austin saying he didn't cheat on his wife. The video is from a private investigator, and the woman is a known prostitute. As Matthew said, we now know he lied to us about not being inside the Armstrong's house the night Savannah was murdered."

"But you already knew he was there that night."

"We knew he was there, not inside the home. Now we know he was, and we've connected him to the trunk itself. That's big Lily. We even have a receipt from when the trunk was purchased, and we've verified that with the seller. The timeline fits with the Armstrong's story. We've got him, Lily. He's our guy."

It sure sounded like it, but something still just didn't sit right with me. "What about the font on the notes? Have you heard anything about that yet?"

He shook his head. "We're still researching. All we know is it's not a standard font found on any word processing software. I've got people checking, but there are thousands of fonts online, and it's taking time to go through them all."

I imagined it would. "When's his bail hearing?"

"Judge will see him late today or first thing tomorrow, but it won't matter. He's not getting bail."

"Why not?"

"Out of towner. Wealthy family. No ties to the area. Too much of a flight risk. Judge won't let him see the light of day until the trial, and he probably won't even see it then."

CHAPTER 7

"*D*o you think I can see him?"

He drummed his fingers on his desk. "Why did I know you were going to ask that?"

I wanted to say because he knew me so well, but I settled for, "Because I'm predictable."

"Or something." He picked up the receiver on his desk and made arrangements. "Fifteen minutes, but that's it."

"Okay. Thank you."

He led me to the jail, cleared me through the electronic security door and set me in the waiting area behind the glass window. I sat on the stiff metal chair and waited until Austin Emmerson came through the door on the other side.

When he saw me, his hardened face softened, and relief washed over him. "Oh, thank God. Someone that believes me."

His expression switched from relief to worry when he saw my stiff posture and reddening face.

"You do still believe me, don't you?"

My momma taught me to always be kind, but at that moment my thoughts weren't kind at all, and I struggled to keep them to myself. "I don't take kindly to liars."

He breathed in deeply and closed his eyes as he exhaled, blowing the air up toward the gray, sterile ceiling. "I deserved that."

I kept my eyes glued to him, waiting to see if he'd continue.

"It's not what you think. I promise."

"Which part? The part where you said you didn't cheat on Savannah, or the part where you said you didn't kill her?"

"Both." He scooted his chair closer to the table and leaned toward the glass window. "Yes, I had sex with a hooker, but it was after Savannah left me. The...the tape was edited or something to leave out the timestamp." He sat back again and dragged his thumb and forefinger down the sides of his face. "I don't know. She didn't show anyone the timestamp on the video though, because if she did, it wouldn't even be an issue. My parents are getting the original, and you'll see. It's after she had the fight with my parents and left for Bramblett."

I didn't support any kind of infidelity, and in my book, even if Savannah had already left, they were still legally married, and that was still infidelity. I knew I thought differently than most people in their twenties, so I tried not to judge. I did however, judge his prints on the trunk. "Your fingerprints were all over the trunk, Austin. The trunk I saw your wife's body in. The trunk you wouldn't have had access to, so care to explain that?"

"I already did, to your boyfriend, but he doesn't believe me."

I crossed my arms over my chest. "Well, why don't you give me a try?"

"You already know I was at my in-laws the night Savannah was killed."

"I know now. What I knew before was that you were outside the home. Two entirely different things."

"I went there to talk to Savannah. I wanted to work things out. That's the whole reason I came to town." He gripped the edges of the table and shook his head. "I knocked on the door, but she didn't answer. I tried a few times because I knew she was home and figured she was ignoring me. You know, maybe she saw my car or something, so I went around back, checked the windows on the side of the house and stuff. I saw the lights were on, and I knocked on the back door too, but she still wouldn't let me in."

"What time was this?"

He shrugged. "I'd had a few at Willy's. Maybe eleven?"

I'd been long gone by then. I motioned for him to continue.

"A few years ago, we came back to town to surprise her parents. You know, just a quick in and out. They weren't home, so Savannah went around back and got the key under the brown planter on the back porch."

I knew exactly what planter he meant. I'd been with Savannah at least a hundred times when she'd done that very same thing.

"So, I checked to see if the key was still there, and it was."

"And you used it to let yourself in."

He nodded.

"Go on."

"Then I called out for her, but she didn't answer, so I checked the house. I thought maybe she was hiding from me or something." He paused and gazed at the gray wall above my head. "I knew what you and Savannah had done, and the place looked great. I saw the sticky notes everywhere, and I read a few of them, mostly the ones on the bookshelves and in the kitchen. I knew about the trunk because she got the same one a month ago. It was a big deal to her."

He paused again and shook his head as if he was replaying something in his mind. "I tried to open it. Unlatched the bolts and everything, but the key wasn't in the lock."

Little alarms buzzed in my head. "Was there a note on the trunk?"

He nodded.

"Was there red paint on it?"

He tilted his head to the side. "Paint? I don't think so. Why?"

I shook my head. "Nothing, forget it."

He continued. "Lily, I could be wrong, but I don't think I am, and that's what I told your boyfriend. I think the trunk in my in-laws' house is ours."

"What? Why?"

"Because when she bought ours, the only one left was the floor model, and it was slightly damaged. Savannah doesn't do scratch and dents. She wants everything to be perfect, so I wouldn't put it past her to switch it out without her parent's knowledge."

I wouldn't either, actually. "Do you have the receipt to prove she bought the last one?"

He laughed. "You're kidding, right? Savannah never saved receipts. Why would she? She never returned anything. That took too much time. She'd just throw it out and buy a replacement."

Wow. I wish I had that life luxury. "Is the other one still at your house?"

"It was when I left to come here. If she's had someone there to move her stuff out since then, I can't say."

"Did she know you were coming to town?"

"No, and I did that on purpose. Savannah is—or was manipulative. If she'd known I was coming here, she'd have moved everything but my clothes out of the house five minutes after I left."

He definitely knew his wife. I had to give him that. "Austin, was the envelope on the door when you got to the house that night?"

"What envelope?"

"The one Savannah left for me."

"There wasn't a note on the door."

"Did you tell all of this to Dylan?"

He nodded and then leaned back in his chair. "But he still

thinks I killed her." He swiped a hand through his short hair. "There's no way I'll make bail. Not in this podunk town."

I narrowed my eyes at him.

He bowed his head. "I'm sorry."

I brushed it off. "You're right. Dylan's already said there's no way the judge will let you out."

He rubbed his palms on his pants. "And it doesn't matter that I'm innocent." His eyes pleaded with mine. "You believe me, don't you?"

I breathed heavily. "If you didn't kill her, then who did?"

He stood and paced the small room. "I don't know. It could be any one of the UGA group. Billy. Heather. Caroline. If I had to pick one, it would be Heather. She never got over what happened. I mean, I get it. I didn't do right by her, and neither did Savannah, but it was a long time ago, and she should have moved on by now. When she threatened her like that at the brunch though, I knew she wasn't right in the head."

"At the brunch? You mean the sorority brunch last month?" Every quarter our sorority pledge class had a brunch get together for the girls in the area. It usually took place in Atlanta, and anyone that could make it, went, except me and Belle. I'd stopped going a few years ago, and Belle rarely went. Neither of us were the typical sorority girls anyway, and the brunches were just a throwback to our college days. Too much make up, too much gossip and way too much food. Been there, done that, and I had no intention of a do over, especially not every quarter.

He nodded. "Heather showed up and it got heated. Told Savannah she stole her life and lit into her big time. Said she'd make her pay for what she did. The rest of the girls had to separate them. Savannah said they told Heather she wasn't allowed back."

"I had no idea any of that happened."

"The thing is, Savannah wasn't the one that started our relationship. I did. I came onto her. She was still with Billy at the time."

I wondered what else I didn't know.

"Yeah, there's a lot about Heather Barrington that your boyfriend doesn't know, but my parents have an attorney on the way, and reasonable doubt is all I need, and I'm pretty sure my attorney will be able to establish that. The three of them all had a reason to want Savannah dead, don't you think?" He nodded. "Yeah, they all did. It's going to be okay. I'll get out of this."

He'd already convinced himself, and he'd also kind of convinced me, too.

～

Belle was gone when I finished talking with Austin, so Dylan offered to drive me home. Since Uber wasn't popular in Bramblett, and I'd have a better chance of seeing the Easter Bunny than a cab, I accepted. I didn't mind the one on one time in my house or in public, but in his car, it felt a bit claustrophobic and a little too close for comfort. I had nowhere to go if the urge to run took over, and that made my fingers tingle and my heart race.

I sat quietly, tapping my left foot while he drove. My quietness didn't go unnoticed. When your ex-boyfriend was a law enforcement officer, those things never did. "You okay?"

I nodded. "Just thinking about some things Austin said."

"Care to elaborate?"

I took the invite and went to town with it. "About the two trunks. I can see Savannah swapping them, and that would explain Austin's fingerprints on the one here."

"That's true."

"And he said the event with the other woman was after Savannah left him, but that the timestamp is missing on the video."

"He told me that also."

"His parents are getting the original video."

"I know."

"And Savannah was already here when he was with that woman."

"Can he prove that?"

I wasn't quite sure. "Well, I met with her the day she got in town. And besides, can't you verify it through her cell phone records or something?"

"There are things we can do, yes." He glanced at me while at the red light. "You're getting pretty good at this, Little Bean."

My heart skipped a beat, and I had to look away. "It's all that crime TV I watch."

"Must be."

Once I'd got my heart rate back to normal, and my house in my line of sight, I faced him again. "Did he tell you about the sorority brunch?

Dylan's eyes shifted from the road to me and back to the road again. "No. What about it?"

"I guess Heather went off on Savannah and blamed her for everything wrong in her life." I filled him in on the rest of the details.

He tapped his forefinger on the steering wheel. "Do you know who was at this brunch?"

"Not off hand, but there's a Facebook group for the pledge class, so I'm sure I can find out."

"Would you mind doing that for me?"

I perked up and straightened my shoulders. "Oh, like be your assistant detective or something?"

"Or something, yes."

"I'm not sure you get what I mean by or something."

He laughed. "We can discuss that later. How's that sound?"

"I'll stick with assistant detective for now." I wasn't sure I was up for any kind of later when it came to Dylan. Not at that moment. I pushed a blond curl behind my ear. "I really don't think he did it."

I watched his chest go up and down. "The evidence says otherwise, Lily."

"Maybe on the surface the fingerprints do, and maybe Austin's dishonesty makes him look bad, but when you dig deeper, the pieces don't fit."

"According to Austin. If he can prove that, we'll see. Until then, we use what we've got."

"What if something else can show even more reasonable doubt? Then what happens?"

He pulled into my driveway. "How about we cross that bridge if we come to it?"

"I think we're there now."

He put his car in park and angled his body toward mine. "Okay. Tell me what you've got."

"I saw Heather with William again this morning, and I called her out on seeing them together."

"I'm not sure how that has anything to do with Austin's part in Savannah's murder."

It didn't exactly have anything to do with Savannah per say. It just wasn't right in my book, and when something wasn't right, that meant it was wrong. "It just shows bad behavior, and this is William, who we now know is a cheater, and Heather, who basically threatened me, so, there's that." I opened the car door.

"Threatened you? Wait. What do you mean she threatened you?"

I explained the conversation I'd had with Heather earlier that day.

He pinched the bridge of his nose. "Why didn't you tell me this earlier?"

"I don't know. The day's just kind of been a big blur, and honestly, it didn't seem all that big of a deal at first. Not until just now, really." I considered everything swirling around in my head at that moment. "Given that I just reported feeling threatened, and you have the note from my door, isn't that cause to check out Heather's computer?"

"I'd need a subpoena to do that."

"Oh. I thought that might create reasonable doubt."

"It's definitely something Austin's attorney could try to use."

"So, what does that mean for your case?"

"It means I've got a lot of work to do, and I'm not sure when I'll be done tonight, but I'd like to come by after work and check on you. Is that okay?"

My heart begged me to say yes. It wanted me to shout it at the top of my lungs, but I knew if I did it would send us down a rabbit hole that could leave me feeling more claustrophobic than any car ever could. "No, Dylan. I don't think that's a good idea."

He pressed the issue. "I won't stop trying, Lily."

"I'm sorry. I don't know what to say." I got out of the car and walked toward my front door. It took every ounce of self-control I had not to turn around and run back to him before I got inside, and when I did, I sat at my kitchen table and cried like a baby. When I finally stopped sobbing, I called my mom and cried all over again.

CHAPTER 8

My mother chided me for not realizing my real problem with Dylan. She figured it out as soon as I told her I'd wanted him to come by later, but it had made me feel closed in like I had in his car.

"Oh sweetie, bless your sweet little heart. Dylan isn't your problem, baby girl. You are. You're just afraid of being dependent on a man again, but you've got to let that go. You don't need a man, and you know that, but it's okay to want him. Those two things are different. When are you going to figure that out?"

What she said made sense, and I realized she was at least partially right. Dylan wasn't entirely responsible for my problem. I did deserve part of that blame, but it wasn't because I was afraid of being dependent on him. I was afraid of getting lost in him again, of losing myself to him. It took me a long time to become the woman I was, and I didn't want to lose her, even for the love of my life.

I explained that to my mom. "Oh honey, let me tell you something. Your pa is sweeter than a box of pralines, but when that man kicks the bucket, you can bet I'll still make it to bowling night because that's what us Sprayberry women do. We keep going, and that's what you'll do with that man of yours, you hear me?"

"Yes, Momma, I hear you."

After she decided she'd settled my Dylan dilemma, I lamented on about my discord with Heather and my concerns about Austin's possible innocence.

"Now you know I've never been a fan of that Savannah, but I sure didn't wish her dead, and I just don't see little Heather Barrington being capable of killing someone. She might have changed a bit in college, but a murderer is always a murderer deep inside their soul honey, and Heather? Well, I just don't see that in her."

"I don't know, Momma. I don't think we ever really know what a person is capable of."

"Maybe not, but I know in my heart that Heather Barrington isn't the killer. I just know."

"Okay, Momma."

"I've got to say though, the good Lord seeks justice in His own way, and I don't know what He'll choose to do in this case, but whatever it is, He'll do right by those that deserve His help. I think you should listen to that man of yours and stay out of it. You don't mess with God, honey."

"I'm not involved, Momma, and I promise, I'm not messing with God."

"Well, I sure hope not. I pray every night I don't have to bury one of my own. Heavens, I can only imagine what the Armstrong's must be going through. And the cost of funerals these days? Goodness gracious, when it's my time, just throw me in one of your pa's old fishing boats, nail a piece of wood over it, and dig me a hole in your backyard. That's all I need. Don't even want a fancy tombstone or anything like that. I'll be dead, so what will I care anyway?"

"Momma, we'll make sure you're properly buried and cared for, I promise."

"Well, you might could get me some nice flowers, plant them around my grave. Maybe some white lilies. They'll remind me of you."

I giggled. "But you'll be dead, so you won't care, remember?"

"'Course I will be sweetie, but I'll be with God, and we'll both be watching."

"Oh. Well then, I'll definitely get you those white lilies."

"Well, now that we've got that settled, I think you ought to go and make it right with Heather. You two have been friends for too long to let a little fit like that come between you."

I'd come to view it as more than a fit, but my mother always saw the brighter side to everything, which was one of the things I loved most about her. Heather threatening me though made it hard for me to want to make things right with her.

Talking with my mother wore me out sometimes, and that conversation was one of those times, so I found a reason to end the call. "Hey, Momma, I've got to run. I've got a client calling about one of those condos on the Redbecker property. Got to earn a living! Love you." I disconnected the call and fell onto my couch, exhausted from the emotional rollercoaster of the day and the added hills of talking with my amazing mother.

Make it right. Her words echoed in my brain all afternoon. I'd wallowed in self-pity in the sanctity of my little bungalow under the guise of working from home while Belle handled things at the office before heading out to the city for a night on the town with Matthew.

I pushed my self pity aside and searched for a reason to believe Heather didn't murder Savannah, to find justification in my mother's push for me to make it right between us. Or maybe I needed validation for the little part of me that believed Heather did wrap her arms around an old friend and choked the life out of her.

No matter what the reason, I needed to find out what I needed to find out.

I checked Facebook for the pledge group of my sorority to see who'd checked in at the last brunch. Several had promised to go but only a few actually checked in. That didn't mean the others didn't attend, but I knew I could talk to the ones that did check in and find out.

I wrote down three names of the girls I knew liked to talk, tended to border on gossipy, but only dipped their toes in the water, never went full-throttle into the lake. The true gossipers were unreliable. I needed to hear the story from my sisters that wouldn't put too much of their own personal spin on it, if that was even possible.

I left messages for two of them and struck gold when my old friend Julia answered.

"Hey girl, what's up? I haven't talked to you in ages." Julia came from the deep south of Mississippi, and even though she lived in Atlanta, she spoke like she'd just hopped off the train from Biloxi.

"Oh, I'm just doing my thing. Listen, I'm calling with some sad news."

"Oh, sweetie, I heard about Savannah, bless her heart. What a terrible way to die. Have you heard anything about her funeral? Of course us girls just have to do something. Maybe we'll have a luncheon in her honor. What do you think?"

"I haven't talked to her parents about the funeral arrangements yet. I know they're in town, but they're keeping to themselves until everything is settled. I think the idea of doing something is lovely. Maybe we could contribute to a charity in her honor or something." I paused to take a breath and ask her about Heather, but she started up again.

"Oh, heavens no. Savannah would roll over in her grave if we gave money to charity. She did not believe in handouts. Why, every time we did a fundraiser, she pitched a fit, bless her heart. She was all, how can you expect people to learn to take care of themselves if you keep helping them? They might could get a job at the McDonalds and rent a room if they need to, she'd say. Oh, gosh." She sniffled. "Oh, dear. Give me a second, honey." She blew her nose. "I just can't believe she's dead. And Austin, arrested for her murder, bless his heart. Who would have thought he'd do that kind of thing? No sir, not me. Raised in a good home, with that kind of money? I can't even imagine what happened to him. It just goes to show, you can provide the best things for your child, but you can't guarantee they won't grow up and be a serial killer, you know what I'm saying?"

Austin wasn't exactly a serial killer. In fact, I wasn't sure he was a killer at all. "Julia, I'm not so sure Austin killed Savannah."

"Well yes, ma'am, of course he did. I heard he was arrested and everything. He is sure in the need of prayer, now, don't you think? And arrested by your ex-boyfriend to bat. Bless your heart, it must be hard having Dylan back in town like that. When I spoke to Heather last, she said he looked mighty fine, like an angel straight from heaven. You know, Atlanta's a big city, and I never did run into him around here. You'd think I would have, but I just didn't."

Goodness, Julia definitely hadn't lost her Biloxi speak. I used her bringing up Heather's name as a segway into my question and to avoid discussing Dylan directly. "When did you talk to Heather last?"

"She's the one that told me about Savannah. Called me the day she discovered her body, bless her heart. She was all tore up about it, too, poor thing."

"Heather told you she found Savannah's body?"

"Yes, ma'am, she did. She told me the whole story. How you had that staging class, which, by the way, I think it just adorable. I'd love for you to come down to the city and give me some tips. My designer is great and all, but she's in her forties and has an old lady vibe, bless her heart. It just doesn't work for me. I'm more of a modernized city girl, you know what I'm saying?"

"Sure, we can chat about that. So, what were you saying about Heather finding Savannah?"

"Oh, yeah, that. She said you had that class and met at Savannah's house, and she didn't want to go, but you know how us girls are curious about that kind of stuff, so she went ahead and went and when she saw that trunk, the one that Savannah suggested her parents get? She has, or had I guess, one just like it. I was at her place two weeks ago and she showed me it. Just beautiful." She made an emm hemm sound. "I wonder what's going to happen to all those beautiful pieces now? Considering that Austin is probably going to spend the rest of his life in jail, bless his heart."

She rambled on, so I interrupted her and gently guided her back to the question I'd asked.

"Anyway, when Heather saw the trunk, she just had to open it, she said, and lo and behold, there was Savannah, stuffed in there like an old forgotten quilt." She sighed. "She said she'd always kind of wished Savannah dead, but seeing her like that, it upset her right good."

I made a decision on the fly to let Heather's story be. It didn't benefit me to tell Julia the truth. "So, you're saying she was upset? Even after what happened at the last brunch?"

"Oh, well, yes, ma'am, that was terrible, and I know Heather was just a mess because of that. Why, she even said so on the phone. But yes, she told me flat out she was tore up about Savannah's death. Said she hadn't had a chance to apologize to her about the brunch incident, but she was planning to. It's just terrible. Come to think of it, I don't know what's worse. Having to live with the guilt of knowing you can't make amends like that or dying without being forgiven."

"I'm pretty sure just dying in general is worse."

She laughed. "Well, of course dyin's worse, but you know what I mean."

I didn't really, but I just let it go. I'd learned to let a lot go with the girls in my sorority, especially the ones that moved up and on. Their world was far different than mine. "Can you tell me what happened at that brunch?"

"Oh, honey, it was B. A. D. Bad. Let me tell you, if I had done what Savannah did to Heather and Caroline, I sure as heck wouldn't be brunching with them now, or even ten years from now. Some things a woman just can't forget, and one of them is stealing your boyfriend, or doing something your momma wouldn't approve of behind closed doors. You know what I mean?"

"I do."

"We just got to consider ourselves lucky that Savannah never set her sights on our men, or else who knows where we'd be right now. Bless her heart, that girl was easier than learning the alphabet."

I figured I'd still be single and right where I was, on the phone with a sorority sister. "Who was the problem at brunch, Heather or Savannah?"

"God bless Heather, she tried to keep her sense about her, but that Savannah, you know how she was. She just wouldn't let it go. She kept pokin' the bear, and pokin' the bear and soon enough, that bear came out fighting, and then food was flying and we were all ducking, and I got eggs benedict on my brand new five-hundred-dollar Donna Karan tunic. Do you know how hard it is to get eggs benedict out of Donna Karan? According to my dry cleaner, it's nearly impossible. Cost me almost one-hundred dollars. I cried like a little girl when I dropped it off. Cried."

I couldn't imagine paying five hundred bucks for a shirt, let alone wearing a tunic, or paying close to a hundred bucks to clean it, but the thought of a food fight did make me smile, until I remembered what it was about. "I was under the assumption Heather started it."

"Oh, no ma'am, she did not. Savannah did. She brought Caroline into it, too. Had her all up in a tizzy about William, she did. It got so bad both of them threatened her. That's when we had to make the decision to not allow them all back. It just wouldn't work, and none of us wanted to pay that kind of money for dry cleaning just one item."

I had no idea Caroline had been involved. "Caroline threatened Savannah?"

"Yes, ma'am, she did. She said if Savannah ever came near William, why it would be the last thing she'd do. Even went as far to say that if any of us came near her husband she'd put us in an early grave. I don't know how much time you spend with her, but she's not the same girl she was at Georgia. Something's broken in that girl now, bless her heart. If I was you, I'd keep your distance. I know Heather had been. She said she'd barely spent any time with Caroline anymore, and if she did, it was only because she felt an obligation to.

"You know, all this talk has me thinking, you've got a whole lot of crazy going on near you, bless your heart. Why don't you come out to the city for a few days? You can stay with me in one of my guest rooms, and we can do a little quick remodel like thing in at my place. You know, spend a little time catching up, and you can work your magic. My husband knows a few movie producers. Maybe he can introduce you to one of them, and you can get your own reality TV show on that do it yourself network or something? You might could be famous."

The last thing I wanted was fame. I liked my anonymous life just fine. "That sounds great, Julia, but I really can't right now. My schedule is full at the moment. How about I call you back later next week and chat again?"

"Oh, sweetie, I would love that. It's been so wonderful catching up with you. We really miss you and Belle at the brunches. Y'all just have to come next time, you hear?"

"Well, do our best. I'll talk to you soon, okay?"

"Okay, sweetie. Ta ta."

Goodness. Julia had good intentions, but I needed a nap after that conversation.

I wandered around the house thinking about that conversation. Not only did I wonder more about Heather's role in Savannah's death, but I considered how Julia portrayed Caroline as even more unstable than she'd appeared, and worried that I should have focused more on her than Heather or William.

As I paced the rooms of my bungalow, I heard each step, the soft smoosh of my bare foot hitting the carpet, the firmer smack of it rolling onto the wood floor of the kitchen. I didn't step on any soggy, slimy dog toys, and I hadn't once been drooled on, or slipped on any wet spots on the floor. No one yelped for my attention. The quiet screamed like a silent alarm, and I realized my little bungalow just didn't feel like home without my crazy little monster crashing around in it. Halfway through the end of the day I threw on a pair of leggings and a t-shirt and walked to doggy daycare.

Two minutes into the walk, I immediately regretted not pulling my hair up into a ponytail. Thick with moisture, the pre-rain air had me set to win first prize in a llama look-alike contest. My blonde curls frizzed out like an 80s southern girl with an Aqua Net addiction. I walked with the lion's mane of frizz wrapped into a ball and held it on the top of my head. When I got onto the main strip in town, I popped into the drug store and picked up a box of hair bands. Sans wallet, I promised to pay for them on my way to work the next day.

One of the best things about living in a small town was the ability to do just that. Pay on my word. They knew I was good for it, and I was. I twisted my hair into the band and went on my way.

I texted Heather as I walked. "I don't like the way we ended our conversation. I'm sorry for my part in it. I'd like to make things right. Can we meet?"

The text was honest. I did feel badly for my part in what

happened but given what Austin had told me and all the things Julia said, I needed to see her again and decide if I believed Heather truly was capable of murdering Savannah, or maybe, if Caroline was instead.

I grabbed Bo, and we headed to the dog park. Even though he was tired, he still had enough energy to bounce around the park with his friends, and it amazed me that he didn't just collapse right there and sleep like the dead.

I checked my phone every few minutes, but Heather hadn't responded. I replayed the conversations over in my head, and that led me to rethinking the events of the last few days, back to when Savannah made her grand entrance into the first day of class.

I focused first on Heather. The hatred in her eyes when Savannah walked into the library conference room, the bitterness in her voice when she spoke. The near pleasure she got when she saw Savannah stuffed into the trunk. The red paint on the sticky notes in the Armstrong's house. Their fight at the pledge class quarterly brunch. Her subtle threat to keep my nose out of her business.

Heather wasn't as sweet as she wanted people to believe, and the way she'd altered her story to Julia made that obvious. She'd carried this hate for Savannah inside of her for so long it grew from a grenade to a cannonball and whether she started it or not, last month at the brunch, it finally exploded.

Yes, Julia said Savannah started it, and while I could see that, I also knew Heather was passive aggressive enough to set the event in motion, and it was quite possible Julia and the rest of the girls just hadn't noticed.

If Julia did call it right, and Heather was the victim, Savannah could have pushed her past her limit, and when given the opportunity, Heather sought true revenge, and that revenge landed poor Savannah inside the trunk at her parent's house.

According to Austin, William cheated on Caroline in college.

Austin wasn't the most credible source, but if he was telling the truth, that could end William's marriage. Caroline's behavior toward Savannah was over the top, and I had no idea what went on behind their closed doors. Had she gone home the first day of class and told William what happened? Did he worry Savannah would spill the beans and tell his wife about their relationship? Could he have killed her because of that?

Seeing William sneaking around town with Heather gave me the willies. Were they doing something behind Caroline's back, too? Did Caroline know? Did she know about Savannah? If she did, was she the one who killed her?

I realized then I had more questions than answers, and the only way to get those answers was to start asking people other than myself those questions.

～

I walked Bo around town for another thirty minutes hoping to hear back from Heather. When I didn't, I decided to drop Bo at home, feed him, and then make a quick run to her house.

Bo ate his food in seconds flat. I sat in awe, praying he wouldn't choke as he inhaled the mini bits of kibble. I'd heard of puppies choking on their food, and though it wasn't common, I still had him eating out of the special puppy bowl designed to slow down dogs eating. I kept it for that reason, but also because while he ate, he spun in tight little circles around it and it was fun to watch.

I let him outside to do his business after he ate and then put him in his crate. He rarely spent time in there, but he didn't mind when he did. He snuggled up on top of his blankets and one of my old UGA sweatshirts—yes, a red one—with his little blue elephant under his front paws, the only toy he hadn't chewed to bits, and snoozed. I switched on the radio for company.

Since Heather still lived with her parents, I fully expected someone to be home. I rang the doorbell but didn't hear it chime, so I knocked. No one answered. Her car sat in the turnaround in the driveway, so I sent her a text.

Five minutes later she still hadn't responded. She's just mad at me, I thought. There's nothing wrong, I told myself. Just in case, I peeked in the front window. The kitchen light was on, but nothing else from what I could see. I tried her cell one more time, but it went straight to voicemail.

I pulled on the front door's handle, but it was locked. I considered walking around to the back of the house and checking the door there, but my gut told me something wasn't right. I trusted my gut, so I waited another few minutes, and when I still hadn't heard from Heather, I hopped back into my car, drove down the street, parked and called Dylan. "Can you come and do one of those wellness checks at Heather's house?"

"A wellness check?"

"Yes, you know, where you go inside and make sure everything's okay."

"I know what a wellness check is, Lily. Why do you think I need to do one at Heather's?"

"I texted her a while ago, and I haven't heard back. I'm at her house now, and her car's here, but she's not answering the door. I even texted her again, and I called her, but my call went straight to voicemail."

"Have you considered that maybe she doesn't want to talk to you? Didn't she tell you to stay out of her business anyway?"

"Yes, but—" I groaned. "You don't understand. We were good friends before. I can't just stop caring about her. Even if I do think she could be a killer." I realized how ridiculous that sounded after I said it. "Would you please just come here?"

"I'm already on my way. I'll be there in two minutes. You're not at the house, still are you?"

"No. I know you would have told me to leave the property, so I did."

"That's my girl. Stay in your car. I see it already."

I glanced in my rearview mirror and saw his vehicle pulling up to the stop sign a block behind me. I stepped out of my car and waited.

"Stay here. I'll text you in a minute," he said as he drove up and then pulled away.

My mouth dropped open. "Oh, heck no," I yelled. I jumped in my car, started it and rode his tail the three driveways to the Barrington's house.

"Why didn't you wait like I told you to?"

"Really?"

He shook his head. "Just stay behind me, okay?"

"Yes, sir."

He shook his head again, but I caught that little twitch on the side of his mouth, and I couldn't help but smile. He saw that I saw and said, "Stop it."

"Stop what?"

"You know what."

I raised my eyebrows and pressed my lips together. Goodness, he was lovely.

He pressed the doorbell.

"Nobody's home. I already tried that."

He widened his stance and ignored me. When no one answered, he knocked on the door.

"Tried that already, too."

He clasped his hands behind his back and waited.

I coughed.

He tipped his head forward and groaned.

"If you look in the window, you'll see the kitchen light is on, but that's about it. Can't you just break down the door or something?"

"I'm not going to break down the door, Lily."

"But it's an emergency. That's why I called you here."

"You called me here for a wellness check."

"Yes, because someone's wellness is an urgent matter."

He wrenched off his hat and grabbed my hand. "Come on," he said, dragging me to the side of the one story house. "Where's Heather's room?"

"On the other side, at the back of the house."

"I'm assuming she has a window?"

I nodded.

"Okay, let's go see if we can see anything in there. Maybe she's asleep, but I doubt it. She's probably out with someone that picked her up. People do that sometimes, you know, not take their cars when they go out. Like when they go on dates, with men."

"Is that a dig or something? Because if so, now is not the time for that. I have been on dates. I've dated. In fact, I went on a date before we—"

He raised his eyebrow. "I didn't mean you and another guy, Lily. I meant you and me."

I blushed. "Oh."

Heather's bedroom curtains were drawn, and the room was dark, but there was a slight glow from the hallway, and I assumed it came from the kitchen light down the hall. The curtains had just enough of a space between them for us to peek inside. Dylan flashed his flashlight in and looked first.

He flipped around, pulled his cell phone from his pocket and called the dispatch operator for the county. "I'm going to need an ambulance to the Barrington house on Route 53."

"What's going on?" I asked. I tried to move around him and look between the curtains, but he wouldn't let me.

"Come on, let' go to the front of the house." He pulled me back toward the driveway.

"She's in there, isn't she? Oh no. What's going on? Is she dead?"

He nodded. "I'm so sorry, Little Bean."

A loud banging interrupted the moment, and Dylan drew his gun from inside the back of his waist. He pushed me against the house. "Stay here." He pointed at me. "And I mean it."

I nodded, my eyes wide.

He aimed his gun in front of him and slipped around the corner of the house. I couldn't hear anything over my pounding heart and short nervous panting, so I crouched down and focused on staying calm. Any attempt at calming myself flew out the window when I heard someone running through the yard next door. I recognized the sounds of shoes crunching down on leaves and sticks breaking under the pressure of pounding feet. I moved toward the edge of the house to try and catch a glimpse of the runner but was afraid to go too far because the original sound had come from that side.

I froze when the neighbor's yard lit up like a football field and an old man screamed, "Who's out there? You'd better get off my property, or I'll shoot."

Dylan responded with his name and title, and the man yelled, "Oh, that's you, Dylan Roberts? How you doin', Sheriff? I knew your pa. What's he been up to these days?"

I wanted to tell the old man to put a lid on it, but I was flat out too scared to speak. Someone had just murdered another one of my friends, and for all I knew, it could have nothing to do with Savannah and her floozy ways, and Belle or I could be next.

CHAPTER 9

*D*ylan set up four deputies to block both sides of the street. He thought that would stop the town gawkers from hanging out to watch the newest tragedy to strike in our small community, but I knew better.

He may have grown up in Bramblett County, but his time in Atlanta flipped the small town switch in his brain to off. The collective of rubberneckers just parked their cars at the road blocks, climbed over them and trekked up to the Barrington's front lawn on foot.

He stepped outside and saw the gathering crowd. "What in God's creation are these people doing?" He placed his hat back on his head, adjusted it to fit just right and talked into the mic on his right shoulder. "Rogers, get the yellow tape and drape it across some trees or something. Someone help him. I want these people out of here. Now. Threaten to arrest them if you have to. This ain't no circus show."

Dylan charged toward one of his deputies and flung his hands around in an emotionally charged conversation. I tried to hear what he said, but other than his obvious frustration, I couldn't figure it out. When he came back to the house, his walk was less determined, almost calm. His brows were furrowed so much the space between them formed two straight lines, and his eyes didn't show strain, but were soft and compassionate and aimed straight for me.

He sat next to me on the porch swing. "How you holding up? Do you need an ambulance? I could call Billy Ray for you."

Billy Ray was very likely on some back road doing the tongue tango with Bonnie. Just the thought of that made my stomach hurt more than it already did. And regarding how I was holding up, well, not all that great, I thought. Aside from my already puffy eyes from crying about him earlier, and the splotchy skin and the rash developing under my nose from it leaking and my rubbing it, I felt like one of the construction trucks at the Redbecker property had dropped a load of bricks on my chest and left it there. Just breathing took miraculous effort. "I'm okay."

The last thing Dylan needed was a train wreck ex-girlfriend losing it on him in the middle of the second murder in less than a week in his county. At that rate, he'd never get officially elected as sheriff.

And then he'd definitely leave me. Again. I lifted my eyes to his and lost it.

He pulled me close, thinking my tears fell for my friend, when my selfish heart cried instead for a future that hadn't even happened. Pull it together Lily, I thought. At least you can still live your life and love a man if you want. Your friend is dead. She'll never have the things she wanted. "Stop being a selfish little thing." I heard those last few words in my momma's voice.

I sat up and left his comforting embrace. I rubbed my raw nose, wiped my eyes—my mascara long gone hours before, and I didn't even care—and dug deep into the pit of my soul for what little strength I had left, and lassoed it up where it belonged. "How about you? Are you okay?"

"Thirty more seconds." His jaw clenched, and the veins in his neck hardened like cords. "If I'd have had thirty more seconds, I could have caught the runner."

I smiled. "So, what's your pa been up to these days?"

He snorted. "What kind of ever lovin' crazy was that? I'm chasin' a perp, and this guy wants an update on my pa?"

I busted out laughing, I just couldn't help myself. In all the days of anxiety, trepidation and death, that was the craziest thing I'd heard, and it hit my funny bone like a baseball player hit a home run, hard and with perfect aim. I couldn't stop laughing, and Dylan laughed right along with me. It was cathartic.

I couldn't tell, and I didn't care, but I would have bet my life savings the people that saw us either thought we were crazy or rude, and I fully expected a call from my momma about proper manners at a crime scene sometime in the near future.

After a few minutes, the laughter subsided, and the serious-ness of the situation set in. "I need to know what's going on in there. Please."

"I know you do, and I promise, I'm going to tell you."

"When?"

"When I'm finished here." He placed his hand on my knee. I gazed at it, suddenly appreciating the strength and steadiness it provided. "Go home, Lily. I'm sending a deputy with you."

"I thought someone was already keeping an eye on me?"

"From a distance, yes. But now I'm keeping someone close by. The killer very likely saw you here and may think you got a glimpse of him. We need eyes on you twenty-four-seven." He squeezed my knee. "And I don't care what you say, I'm staying on your couch again tonight. I'll be there as soon as I can."

I didn't argue.

~

Bo's bottom and extra-long tail waggled and shook like he hadn't seen me in months. Boxers typically had their tails snipped, but I couldn't do it. He looked mostly like a Boxer, but there was another dog or two in his DNA, and whatever it was, I was confident the tail had been used as a weapon. I'd already lost three glasses and an ugly porcelain knickknack an elderly client gave me because he'd whipped his tail into them and sent them crashing into pieces on the ground.

Being greeted by a big lug of a puppy with sloppy wet kisses was the best medicine in the world. I unhooked his crate door and sat on the ground, my arms open and ready for his love assault.

I didn't mind the kisses except for the under tongue part. When the under part of his tongue slid upwards on the reverse part of the kiss, it bordered on slimy and admittedly, the ick factor tipped the scales, but it wasn't Bo's fault. For him, the lick was an expression of love, so I suffered through the under tongue slop and enjoyed the affection. Sometimes it felt like the world's problems could all be solved if everyone just sat on their kitchen floor and let an oversized puppy shower them with wet kisses.

After a few minutes and a slimed face, I had an overwhelming urge to purge the effects of the day from my body and from my soul, if at all possible. I attended to Bo's needs and then ran a bath for myself.

I wouldn't call myself a germaphobe, but I did take issue with just stepping into a bath tub full of water after spending the day living. Wasn't that basically bathing in your own dirt? I didn't bathe to clean myself. I bathed for an emotional cleansing, but to clean the inside, I first needed to clean the outside. So, while the tub filled, I took a shower. Thankfully, it wasn't something I did often, and I could still afford to pay my water bill.

It was already late, and I didn't want Dylan to come over

while I bathed, so I kept my phone nearby. Plus, I'd turned off all the lights and lit a few vanilla scented candles to help me relax. I imagined my dark house, me not answering my phone or texts and then him thinking the deputy outside doing nothing with my house in such a state. Dylan would probably freak out, break my door down and find me naked as the day is long in my bath tub.

I blushed just thinking about it.

The warm, bubbly water and the vanilla scented candles calmed my nerves but not my brain. I couldn't get Heather's death off my mind. Dylan promised to tell me what happened, which in and of itself was unusual, so I knew that meant something. And he set up another deputy to watch over me, and he insisted on staying at my house again, so whatever happened to Heather must have had something to do with Savannah's death.

Which meant he'd arrested the wrong person.

Austin couldn't have killed Heather, not from the county jail. And if he didn't kill her, but the two murders were somehow connected, then that meant he didn't kill his wife, either.

If Austin wasn't the killer, who was? What connected Savannah and Heather and maybe even Austin together that could justify two murders?

My mind circled back to both William and Caroline.

A loud pounding on my bathroom door sent me flying five feet into the air. I scrambled out of the tub, grabbed my towel and wrapped it around my parts no one needed to see.

Before I could ask who it was, the pounding started again, and Belle screamed, "Lily, are you in there? You better be okay, or I'm going to bust this door down." Something smacked the door and she groaned. "Or at least I'm going to try." Something crashed into the door again. I had a feeling it was her body.

I secured the towel under my right arm and unlocked my bathroom door, just as Belle charged toward it. She sailed past me and came to a sliding halt right before making contact with the side of my bathtub. I flipped on the overhead light. "What in heaven's sake are you doing?"

She threw herself at me and pulled me into a bear hug, then immediately disengaged and blanched. "Oh, ick. You're all wet."

"Of course, I'm all wet. I was taking a bath."

She dropped the lid on my toilet and took a seat. "Don't ever do that to me again, you hear me?"

"Clean my body? Uh, okay, but you're not going to like that in the office."

She smiled. "Matthew told me about Heather, and I've been texting and calling you the whole way back from Atlanta. Why haven't you answered your phone?"

I grabbed my phone off the side of the tub and checked it. "Oh." I wiggled it at her. "I guess it died. I'm sorry. I didn't know."

Her eyes bulged. "You didn't know? Miss, I Double Check Everything Before I Leave the House, let her cell phone die and had no idea? After two of our friends have been murdered in less than a week?" She leaned back onto the toilet tank and then quickly straightened, turned around and looked at it.

I rolled my eyes. "Yes, it's clean." Belle had bigger germaphobe issues than me every day of the week.

Her face reddened. "Just checking." She leaned back on it again. "Anyway, you scared the daylights out of me. Don't do that."

"May I see your phone please? I need to text Dylan in case he's tried contacting me."

She handed me her cell, and I let him know I had to charge my phone.

Bo came in and licked my leg.

"How about you take Bo into the kitchen and give him a t-r-e-a-t so I can get dressed?"

"Fine. But hurry. I want to hear what happened."

"Oh, I have a lot to tell you."

Belle slumped into the back of my couch. "I can't believe it. Caroline."

"I know."

"Or William."

"Take your pick." I patted Bo's head, but my eyes were stuck in stare mode. "I don't know which one, but either makes sense."

She sat forward. "But we don't know if Caroline knows about William and Savannah, right?"

"Right."

"And anything between William and Heather is—or was—just speculation on our part."

"Yes, but that doesn't mean it didn't happen."

"True, but he has been acting ugly lately."

"Definitely."

"But then again, Caroline's been a bit on the crazy side, so we can't just shove that under the table."

"Nope. No shoving on my part."

"But if you think about it, who's got more to lose here?"

"What do you mean?"

"If any of this stuff about William and Savannah and Heather is true, who's got more skin in the game, him or her?"

"William, of course. If he did cheat on Caroline with Heather, then his marriage is definitely over, and if she does find out he cheated on her with Savannah, with the way she's talked about it lately, I'm pretty sure that would end their marriage, too."

"I'm right there with you, so if I were a gambling woman—"

"Which you're definitely not."

"Which I'm definitely not, but if I were, I'd have to put my chips on William, not Caroline. He's definitely got the cards stacked against him in this one."

I cocked my head and when it hit me, my mouth dropped

open. "Oh, my gosh. You're watching crime TV shows now, aren't you?"

She cleared her throat. "Maybe once or twice."

"Oh, sweetie, you are so busted from here to Sunday."

"I'm dating a law enforcement officer. I have to keep up with his world, you know."

I laughed. "Dylan told me reality is a lot different than what they show on TV. Half that stuff isn't even possible, and most crimes aren't solved in less than a day."

"If we were solving them, they would be."

"Darn straight."

Dylan responded to my text on Belle's phone. "He said he's on his way." She wiggled her eyebrows. "Maybe I ought to scoot on out of here and give you two a little privacy. You know what I mean?"

I threw a throw pillow from my couch at her. "Get on out then, and let me get to my business."

She jogged to my door, said, "You go girl," and giggled as she closed the door behind her.

"I didn't mean that how it sounded," I hollered, but she just waved her hand behind her and kept walking.

CHAPTER 10

I poured Dylan a tall glass of ice cold sweet tea while Bo covered his face with doggy kisses. His lips were closed tight, but in the shape of a half moon, so I knew he didn't mind. Bo had Dylan on his back on the floor, his colossal sized paws bounding up and down on Dylan's chest. I ordered him to stop, but he kept playing. Dylan laughed, and Bo took that opportunity to stick his tongue directly into Dylan's open mouth.

I laughed. "Ew. I think that means you're going steady now."

He grabbed Bo's paws and lifted the mini-monster off him, moving him onto the ground. When he sat up, he patted Bo's head. "Sorry buddy, but you're not my type."

Bo snuggled up next to him, and Dylan pointed to me. "See your momma over there? That's the woman I intend to marry. Besides, I think I saw a French Poodle at doggy daycare eyeing you big time buddy, so how 'bout we stick to just friends?"

I couldn't help but laugh, even as a bolt of—I don't know what—shot through my body and left my limbs tingling. "Here, drink this." I shoved the sweet tea at his face, pretending I hadn't heard his marriage comment.

We locked eyes, and I saw something in his I'd never seen before. I saw my heart. "Thank you," he said.

I moved to the couch pretending we didn't just have that moment. "So, what's going on?"

He sat near me, and even though he'd spent the day working, I still caught a hint of the fresh soap he'd used since college. I breathed in through my nose just to keep smelling it.

He sighed. "It was a long day."

I leaned closer to him and breathed in his manly, soapy scent, letting it swirl around in my nose, taking me back to high school and the beginning of college, and just last week, where I felt safe, and happy and loved.

"Lily?"

I realized I'd closed my eyes and inhaled deeply. "Yeah, sorry."

The side of his mouth twitched. "Yes, it's the same soap. Why don't you just buy yourself a bar of it so you can smell it when I'm not around?"

The tops of my ears burned, and I backed away. "I..I…what are you talking about? Soap? What soap?"

"You used to do that all the time, you know. Smell me like that? You think I didn't notice? You even did it last week. The first thing I did when I came back to town was get that soap because I knew it was your favorite. I may be good looking, but I ain't stupid." The side of his mouth twitched again.

I pulled my knees up to my chest. "You knew I…I—"

"Liked the way I smell? Yes, I knew. I know, and I think it's kind of cute."

That sounded so much less creepy than what I thought.

He scooted closer, tilted his head to the side and stretched his neck toward me. "Here, put your nose right here."

I backed up again and almost fell over the side of the couch. "Uh, no. That's okay."

He laughed. "Darn. I thought I'd got you with that one."

I smacked his arm. "Nice try, buddy." That's all it took for me to get my head on straight again. "Okay, seriously, what's going on?"

"You might have been right about Austin."

I jumped from the couch. "I knew it. He didn't kill Savannah. I just knew it." I jumped up and down like a frog on steroids.

He sat back with his arms folded. "Let me know when you're finished."

I froze. "Oh, sorry." I sat back down and stayed still, except for my foot, which wouldn't stop tapping on the floor.

"We aren't sure yet, but we think Heather was probably strangled, though we believe whoever killed her wants us to think she poisoned herself. Initially we thought it might be a copycat thing, but we don't think it was."

"I'm confused. She poisoned herself, but she was strangled, too?"

"No, we think she was strangled, but we believe the killer wants us to think she overdosed on drugs. That she committed suicide. At least that's what the note says."

"You found a note?"

"Yes, and that's why we don't think it's a copycat. I'll explain, but first, I'd like you to tell me exactly what you did when you got to Heather's."

"Pretty much what you did. I rang the doorbell and when no one answered, I knocked and then I looked in the window, saw the light was on and got worried, so I drove down the street like you told me to do after Myrtle Redbecker was murdered and called you."

"And you should be glad you did."

"Because?"

"Because it looks like you got there while the killer was there."

The hairs on my arms stood. "You mean, the killer could have seen me?"

"Or heard you. Either way, you scared him—"

"Or her."

"Or her, away, and he—or she—dropped the note on the floor in the hallway. I don't know what he—or she—intended to do with it, but I don't think dropping it in the hallway was the plan. I think the note ended up on the floor because the killer heard you at the door, got scared and rushed to finish the job."

"What did the note say?"

"It was a suicide note. From Heather."

"Oh." I shook my head to clear out the fog. "But you said you don't think she committed suicide."

"No, we don't. We think the killer wrote the note and wants us to think it's from Heather."

"Oh. I get it."

"The thing is, we know she didn't. We just have to wait for the autopsy report to say for sure."

"How do you know?"

"For one, like Savannah, there are similar marks on Heather's neck, but that's not all. When a woman commits suicide, she's most likely to do it through self-poisoning—or drug overdose, and when she does that, it's either in her own bed, or in the bathtub, with the added benefit—for lack of a better term—of drowning. It's a meticulous, planned act, and they're usually well-prepared. Most often, there isn't a note, but when there is, it's not just tossed on the floor in the hallway. It's left some place where the person knows it will be seen, and it's not usually next to the victim. It may be on the nightstand, but usually they leave it some place outside the room where they commit the act, so the person that does find them finds the note first and has a chance to prepare themselves for what's coming."

I didn't know any of that, and to hear Dylan talk with such knowledge and compassion about it made me admire him more. "Okay, so the note on the floor is reason enough to think Heather didn't commit suicide?"

"That's not all. Heather was on the floor along with a bottle of spilled pills. I won't go into too many details, but the position of her body wasn't one typical of someone that overdosed on pills and laid down to die. She'd either collapsed, fallen or been dropped there. Sure, I can see the pills on the floor. She could have had the bottle in her hand and fallen asleep on the bed, but not on the floor, not just standing there. It doesn't happen like that. Could she have taken them somewhere else and wandered into the room and fallen? Yeah, sure, but it's unlikely. Doesn't fit the typical suicidal M.O. of a woman." He paused, took a deep breath and released it. "Does that make sense?"

"I think so."

"But none of that is the kicker. The kicker is the note."

"Why? What did it say?"

"It's not what it said. It's the font. It's the same one as the other notes."

"Have you been able to find the font online yet and trace it to an owner?"

He shook his head. "Not yet, but we're close. Maybe another day or two and we should be able to."

"Oh, my gosh. Then Austin really didn't kill her, did he?"

"I don't believe he did."

"I knew it."

"How many times do you want to say that?"

"About another ten or so, maybe." I winked. "Or more."

"But you thought it might be Heather, didn't you?"

I sighed. "Except that's changed, too. Other than because of the fact that someone killed her, I mean."

"How do you mean then?"

"Because the more I think about it, the more I think William or Caroline could have killed Savannah."

He pulled his left leg up and rested the side of his calf over his right thigh. "But what about Heather?"

I explained the theory as Belle and I saw it.

"I have to admit, Little Bean, you're really learning your stuff.

I guess all that crime TV is paying off." I wasn't sure, but I think one of his teeth sparkled when he smiled.

"You are a big jerk, and besides, this was a lot more Belle than me, though I was pretty much there already. I just hadn't said it all out loud."

He laughed. "I'm serious, really. I think you two might be onto something here."

"Really? Took you long enough." I flung my hair back and batted my eyelashes. I'd gone for sexy and confident, but Dylan laughed, so I knew I'd missed the mark. "So, are you going to let Austin go?"

"Not yet. There's still enough evidence to hold him, so we're going to do that until we can guarantee another killer can be brought to trial."

I felt bad for Austin. "Why? So you can still send him to prison if you can't pin the crime on someone else?"

"No. If I release him, then the killer might know we're onto him and—"

"Or her."

"Or her. Now I understand why you keep saying that. And we want the killer to get lazy and comfortable, to think it's all good and he—or she—doesn't have to worry."

"Oh, that makes perfect sense. So, what happens now?"

"First, I need you to promise not to tell anyone what I've told you. I shouldn't be discussing this with you in the first place, but given the fact that this is the second friend of yours to be killed in a matter of days, I thought you should know. It's a little too close for comfort Lily, and you and Belle need to be careful."

"What do you mean? Like we could be in danger, too?"

"I know you think Heather and Savannah are connected because of Austin, but have you considered other factors? Things that might connect you and Belle to them?"

"The thought has crossed my mind."

"All of you have been friends since you were kids. You went

to school together, to the same college. You were in the same sorority. There's a connection there, Lily. We just have to figure out what. And until we do, both you and Belle, and even Caroline, aren't safe."

When he put it like that, I understood why he wanted to stick close to me. "So, you want to be around me because you're worried something's going to happen to me?"

"Yes." He pressed his fingers into his forehead. "No. I mean, yes and no. I am worried that something's going to happen to you, yes. And yes, I want to be around you to keep you safe, but I also want to be around you because I just want to be around you, you know? I enjoy being with you, Lily. I always have."

Don't cry Lily. Do. Not. Cry. His eyes were warm and caring, and I just wanted to climb into them and spend the rest of my life there.

He spoke barely above a whisper. "I don't know what I'd do if something happened to you."

I nodded, because if I spoke, I would have blubbered all over my couch, and it was only six months old. I didn't want to stain it.

"So, here's what we're going to do. I've got a friend in Atlanta who owns a security company, and he's sending out a guy tomorrow to put cameras up here, at Belle's and at your office. The cameras are accessible through any laptop but also on an app, so Matt and I will have access to them, along with you and Belle, of course. That way we'll be able to keep an eye on your place, so if someone does try to do something and our deputy is disabled or doesn't catch it, we will."

"You're going to be watching me on camera twenty-four seven?"

"That sounds a lot worse than it is. The cameras will be outside, not inside, so it's not like we'll be watching you when you're in your nightie or something." Both of our faces turned red.

I giggled. "My mother says nightie."

"Isn't that what it is?"

"Well, technically, I guess, but that's not what people our age call it."

"Oh really? What do people our age call it then?"

"Flannels or sweats and a t-shirt."

He rolled his eyes. "Oh. Gotcha."

I giggled again. "Actually, I think I got you."

"You've had me since I was seventeen."

I swallowed hard.

He brushed a flyaway hair from my face. "So, you okay with this?"

I twisted my fingers together and lifted just my eyes toward him. "You're going to stay here until this is over, right? In the guest bedroom, of course."

"I've got a week's worth of clothes packed in a bag in the car, Little Bean."

CHAPTER 11

*B*oth Dylan and Matthew suggested we continued with business as usual the next day and that included holding the decluttering class. Neither Belle nor I wanted to, but we both agreed it made sense. She and Matthew had come over first thing in the morning. Belle had thrown her hair up in a bun and tossed on her go-to yoga pants and multi-colored sweatshirt with white, girly, bubbly letters that read, I'm All That and More. The sweatshirt had seen better days in its fifteen or so years, but it was her favorite, and I knew she wore it because it made her feel safe.

I eyed her outfit and pulled my chin into my neck. "Is that what you're wearing to class?"

She pretended to be insulted. "Why darlin', it took me all night to plan this outfit. Are you sayin' you don't like it?"

The boys watched and played along.

"I think it's stunning," Matthew said.

Dylan shrugged. "It's not bad, but I'm more of a skirt and stilettos guy."

I glanced at my dark jeans and sleeveless top and noted my

inadequate attire. "Well, I'm sure Henrietta or Bonnie will gladly change into something more fitting to your tastes."

Belle laughed. "He'll have to fight Old Man Goodson and Billy Ray for their affections, though."

"I think I can take them."

"Isn't Billy Ray the volunteer paramedic?" Matthew asked.

Matthew was new in town and still getting a handle on the who's who and the what's what.

"Yep," Belle said.

"He's old."

"I think a better word would be seasoned," Belle said.

"Or maybe matured?" I added.

"More like past his prime, but hey, if you think you need help taking he and this Old Man...what's his name?"

"Goodson," we all said collectively.

"Taking he and this old man Goodson down, I'm happy to help."

We all laughed, and though I felt bad for doing so at the expense of two kind men, it was in good hearted fun, and Belle and I needed the light mood. Knowing we might be at risk weighed heavily on our hearts, and our hearts were already heavy from losing our friends.

Adulting was hard. Why we spent our youth rushing to grow up and wanting it so badly made no sense. Sometimes, I longed for a do-over.

Belle changed into her work attire, a more fitting outfit of dark jeans and a light colored cami with a matching button down cardigan sweater. We fixed our hair, applied limited makeup and returned to the kitchen and to two men on their phones doing sheriff stuff.

Dylan disconnected his call and smiled at me. "So, you two know what to do, right?"

I nodded. "Act as though you haven't told us anything and be upset. Which, that last part at least, is true."

"You understand why you're doing this, though?" Matthew directed his question to Belle.

"Yes, of course. No one needs to know what's going on with the investigation. We don't want to put ourselves at unnecessary risk, so on and so forth."

Matthew furrowed his brow. "You could take this a little more seriously, Belle."

She huffed. "I am taking this seriously. I'm the one that suggested we trap the killer, but no. You two don't want to do that."

I raised my hand like a child in school. "Uh, I'm with them on this one. Sorry."

She pouted. "Traitor."

"If that's what you think, I'm fine with that."

"There's a safe way to do this, and we're doing it that way. We've already had two people killed. I'm not going to lose anyone else, no matter who it is," Dylan said.

"I just think we could end this faster if we had a different plan," she said.

"We don't have a plan," Matthew said. "In fact, there is no we in this. There is a Bramblett County Sheriff's Office, and there is you and Lily, but there isn't a we when it comes to a plan. You're doing what the sheriff's office asks because your other option is jail time."

He had this authoritative tone to his voice, a booming, strong tone that made me want to stand up straighter and say yes, sir. It bordered on militaristic, and it impressed me. "Belle, he's right. We have to do what they say, so no funny business, okay?"

She held her hands up in surrender. "No funny business from me, I promise. I think this is wrong, but hey, I'm a real estate agent, not a cop, and I don't watch a whole lot of crime TV, so clearly, I don't know what I'm talking about."

Matthew caught my eye, and I whispered, "She'll be fine. She's just scared."

"I heard that," she said.

"I made sure you did."

"Our guys from Atlanta will be at your office in a few hours. Can I have the code to give them to let them in?" Dylan asked.

"The code's easy. It's our street address. We haven't changed it since we got the new keypad lock last month," Belle said.

Dylan lectured us on how dangerous that was.

"Hey, blame her, not me. I keep telling her we need to change it. She keeps forgetting."

"It's true. I do, but I promise, we'll do it after class today."

The guys left in their department registered vehicles, making sure we saw the two deputies assigned to us hanging out nearby, and Belle and I headed out for our day. I walked Bo and then dropped him off at daycare and drove to Millie's to pick up the breakfast order for class, though I had to have Millie reduce the order again since Heather definitely wouldn't be there.

"Such a shame," Millie said.

I pushed back a tear developing in the corner of my right eye. "I still can't believe it."

"Such a talented artist, that girl. May she rest in peace." Ellie Jean appeared behind me and rested her hand on my shoulder. "How're you holding up sweetie?"

"I'm okay, Ellie Jean. A little shaken up, but life goes on and it's best to let it, you know? I think she'd want that."

"I'm sure she would."

Millie hollered toward the kitchen. "Someone bring me out one of those scones I just took out of the oven, right quick. I got someone that could use a little pick me up." She pulled one of her pink Millie's Café treat boxes from under the counter and put it together. "I just made some new scones. You'll love 'em. Fresh batch, right out of the oven, too. You seeing Belle today? I'll give you one for her, too. Nothing's better at healing a wounded heart than a sweet treat. And I'll tell you a secret, it's got chocolate in it."

My mouth watered. "There's definitely something to say for chocolate healing a broken heart, so I will definitely take you up on the offer, and for Belle, too." I dug in my bag for my wallet. "How much do I owe you?"

"Oh, sweetie, don't you dare try and pay me a dime, you hear? I'd be insulted, and you don't want to insult the woman that makes your coffee and sweet tea every morning. Why, I might just give you decaf one morning for revenge." She winked at me, and I laughed.

"You sure, Millie? I don't mind paying for it."

"'Course I'm sure, honey. That's what we do here, you know that." She handed me the bag and the other items for the class. "You sure you got all this?"

"I think so."

"Ellie Jean, you might could help her with that tumbler, right?"

"Was planning on it, Millie. Once you get me my coffee, that is."

She poured her a cup, added some sugar and cream, topped it with a lid and handed it to her. "It's on me since you're helping our Lilybit here."

"Thank you, darlin'."

Ellie Jean and I walked to the library and talked about what happened to Heather.

I asked her how she'd already heard. "It's not even nine o'clock."

"People talk in Bramblett County Georgia, honey, and word travels fast. There's a site online that lets you listen to dispatch calls and such all over the country. If your county or city is on the system, all you have to do is tune in, and you can hear everything going on." She held open the library door for me. "Haven't you noticed the size of the crowds at all the recent tragedies? You know why that's happening, don't you?"

"Because it's Bramblett County, and it's always happened here."

"Yes, it's always happened here, but that's not why. It's because of the Internet and on account of that website that lets us all listen to the dispatch center for the county." The door closed behind us, and Ellie Jean put her own items on the main desk inside. "Why, I've even downloaded the app to my cellular phone. We've got a Facebook page and everything. Once word gets put on there, you can't stop it from spreading like wildfire."

What website?"

"Goodness, if you young people didn't spend so much time taking those self-portraits, you might know what's going on in the world. It's called broadcastify, and it's got all kinds of dispatches from all over the country. You ought to check it out."

I did feel a little out of the loop and a tad scolded by Ellie Jean, but I hadn't taken a selfie in God only knew how long, so I had that going for me. I wondered if Dylan knew about the website? "I'll definitely check it out."

She set the items down in the conference room. I thanked her for her help, and she asked if she could sit in with us sometime later that day. "I've got an appointment to run to right quick, but I'd love to talk to you about listing my house. I'm thinking about buying me one of those condos on the Redbecker property. Figured I could use a lesson or two on cutting the clutter prior to putting my place up for sale."

"Oh, that would be wonderful. I'd love to help you with listing your place when you're ready."

"I might just take you up on that. Maybe you could come by and check it out? Tell me what I need to do to get it ready?"

"I'm sure we can make arrangements for that. How about we set something up in the next day or two?" I set the new class paperwork out for the three remaining students, even though I wasn't sure any would show up. "I just want to finish up the class and catch up with some things at the office before I add anything to my schedule."

"Sounds like a plan. Now let me get moving, and I'll be back in a bit. My assistant is good, but she never opens the way I like, so I want to make sure some things are attended to before I leave."

Belle came in a few minutes later, dropped her things on the conference room table and gave me a strange look.

I returned the look and asked, "What?"

"Wait for it."

A wobbly Caroline came in hanging onto William's arm. He must have dressed her because even though we lived in a small county a lot of the city folk referred to as redneck, Caroline Abernathy would never be seen in public in a pair of faded, ripped blue jeans—and not the kind currently in fashion—and a Taylor Swift t-shirt. Never.

I held out my arms, worried she might fall on me. "Uh, is she alright?"

Belle leaned against the table and watched. The corner of her upper lip raised up in a snarl; a dead giveaway to her displeasure. Belle never did well at hiding her emotions.

William set Caroline in a chair. Actually, he dumped her in the chair. She landed with a thud, sliding down the back of it in a boneless, jelly-like mess. "She will be in about thirty minutes or so." He pressed the palm of his hand into his forehead. "Listen, I hate to do this to you, but I…I got work to do. I can't babysit her right now, and I know it's a lot to ask, but can you guys watch her? She's all tore up about Heather, and I didn't want to leave her alone. I promise she'll be okay in a bit, once the meds clear her system." He glanced down at her. "And that…that can't be much longer, I don't think. My ma, she gave them to her late last night, but they've got to wear off soon."

"What in the devil's carnation is wrong with that child?"

Henrietta made her grand entrance spouting off, sans filter, as always.

Her sidekick followed on her tail. "She's been partyin' till the cows come home, and I don't think they made it home just yet."

"Ladies, I'm not sure you're aware of what happened to one of our classmates last night, but—"

Henrietta interrupted me. "'Course, we're aware. We're old, but we ain't dead. Besides, I'm dating me a volunteer paramedic. I got connections."

Belle raised her right eyebrow and glanced my direction.

"You're dating Billy Ray?" I pointed to Bonnie. "I thought you were dating him?"

"I was. We switched."

Henrietta stuck out her womanly parts and wiggled them. The effect was wasted in her orange and green potato sack styled dress, but I got the point. "I was a bit too much woman for Old Man Goodson."

Belle choked but covered it with a cough.

"And Billy Ray didn't see my finer points," Bonnie said.

I was afraid to ask what finer points she meant.

"And what are those?" Belle asked.

Ack. I should have known she'd go there.

"Sweetie, some things a lady doesn't discuss in public."

Thank you, Lord.

Henrietta laughed. "Don't let her fool ya. I got me those same finer points. She just likes to pretend hers are better."

William took that as his cue to leave. Frankly, I wished I could have done the same thing. "Okay, so we're good?"

Even though I thought Caroline might have murdered two people, in that moment I honestly just worried about my friend. I sat next to her. "Caroline, are you okay?"

"Hey." She dragged the long a sound when she spoke. "I'm good, Lily. So good." She raised her right hand to my face and dragged her fingers down my cheek. "You're so pretty. Do you know how pretty you are?"

William interrupted our bonding moment. "I'll be back to pick her up when y'all are done, unless you can drop her off after?"

Belle stepped in. "We'll handle your wife. You go do what you gotta do. Cover your tracks or whatever."

The harshness in Belle's tone was a figurative slap across William's face that left an embarrassing red mark draped across his ego. His eyes hardened, and his lips steeled into a straight line. When he caught me watching him, his face went blank.

"We got her, William. Don't worry," I said, hoping to ease the sting of Belle's words.

His expression softened when he looked at me. "Thanks, Lily. I appreciate it." He left the conference room.

I glared at Belle. "Can you step outside for a moment, please?"

She returned my glare with equal furor. "Right."

Henrietta clapped. "Oooh wee. This is gettin' good."

Bonnie clapped, too. "There's gone be a cat fight."

Both ladies, already sitting in their chairs, heaved themselves up and once they'd caught their balance, moved toward the door.

I rubbed the back of my neck. "There's no cat fight coming. We're just going to chat for a moment." It was true, but it didn't mean we weren't a bit annoyed with each other.

We stepped into the hallway. I closed the conference room door and held up my finger just as Belle opened her mouth to speak. I waited a few seconds and then quickly opened the door and both Henrietta and Bonnie fell down in the process. I knew they'd be there, ears shoved against the hollowed wood trying to snoop in on our discussion. Belle laughed, and it eased the tension building between us.

I'd almost reached my limit. It had been a long few days. "Come on you two, haven't you ever had a stressful situation in your lives?"

They both scoped out the floor, refusing to make eye contact with me as if they'd been scolded, but at least they nodded.

"We've just lost two of our friends and both in tragic ways. Would you mind giving us just a minute or two to work through some things together?"

Bonnie glanced at Henrietta. "You'd be a hot mess if someone knocked me off."

"I sure would, but I bet you'd be carted off to the looney bin if it was me in that trunk."

"Not if Billy Ray was doing the carting. He'd probably take me back to his place for a little fun first."

"Oh, darlin', he'd be such a mess himself, he'd be lying in the ambulance next to you."

They walked back into the conference room, and I shut the door behind them. I hugged my friend. "Are you okay?" I knew when Belle stressed, the stress came out in a few different ways, and one of them was anger. I wiped a tear from her face.

"Part of me wants to tie Caroline up and get her to admit what she's done, but the other part of me sees her in there like that, and I just can't imagine her being capable of killing Savannah or Heather, you know?"

"I know."

"And then of course, there's William. Letting his mother drug his wife up like that and then bringing her here and dumping her in that conference room like she's a bag of books for donation? Makes him look more like a heartless killer than her, that's for sure."

"He seemed genuinely concerned and definitely stressed. I was surprised, actually, and he didn't give me an attitude."

"Well, he gave me one. I had half a mind to tell him what I really think of him."

I thanked God she hadn't. "We have to do what Dylan and Matthew said. We can't jeopardize the investigation."

She played with her long, dark hair. "I know. It's just hard. I'm conflicted."

"Trust me, I'm there, too." I fixed her hair for her. "This is going to be over soon and then our lives will be back to normal, I'm sure of it."

"By normal, do you mean you'll straighten things out with Dylan?"

I looked away. "I don't know if that's possible, but we'll see. That's all I can say right now." I hugged her again. "Now, can we go and pretend everything is fine and dandy and let Henrietta and Bonnie amuse us some more? I could really use the laughs."

"They are hysterical, aren't they?"

"Very much so."

~

Caroline came out of her drug induced fog sometime over that next hour, and Ellie Jean did eventually stop into the class and sit a spell. Since the class lacked consistency from the start, we reviewed the previous lessons in more detail than expected, and I used other client photos and various websites to provide detailed examples. I decided viewing photos of the Armstrong's home was inappropriate and in poor taste.

Once Caroline's brain cleared, nice Caroline disappeared, and ugly Caroline showed up. During a quick break, we checked the Internet to see what kind of drugs would cause agitation when a person came off them. The sites said that Caroline's attitude wasn't unusual, but I still wondered if the ugliness was due to the drugs or the fact that she was a cold blooded killer.

Before class started I leaned more toward William as the killer, but after seeing his palpable concern for his wife, and watching Caroline behave with such nastiness, I questioned that thought.

"Great." I clicked the Internet off on my laptop. "We still aren't any closer to knowing if she did it or not."

"Did what?" Caroline asked.

I hoped she wasn't behind us while we'd Googled about the drugs. "Someone sent me, well, Bo really, one of those monthly dog boxes, and I think it was my mom, but I'm not sure." I'd just committed a double sin. Not only had I lied, but I lied about my mother. I instantly regretted it, and I prayed God would understand and forgive me. I knew my mother wouldn't, so I also vowed never to speak of it, even with Belle.

"I told her it probably was," Belle said.

"Well, of course it was. That woman has coddled you since the day she gave birth to you." The minute the words came out of her mouth her hand flew up and tried to stuff them back in. "Oh, heavens, I am so sorry. I don't know what's come over me lately. I am so sassy, and I don't mean it."

"It's 'cause you got that drug addiction," Bonnie said.

"Emm hmm," Henrietta added. "My Uncle Cornelius—we called him Cornie for short—he had himself a liking for moonshine. Too much of a liking, let me tell you, and when he ran out, that man was meaner than a snake. He got so ugly, the whole town stopped serving him. One night, he just couldn't take it no more, and he done shot everyone dead."

Bonnie threw her hand up in the air. "Now don't you believe a thing Henrietta says. If that woman's mouth is open, you can bet she's lying."

Belle smirked. "I've never heard anything about the whole town being shot dead."

"That's 'cause it wasn't this town. It was up yonder." She pointed behind her. "North of us."

She'd pointed south.

Belle pointed where Henrietta had and winked at me. "Up north where?"

"Houston Beech."

"I've never even heard of Houston Beech," I said.

"That's because my Uncle gone and shot the whole town dead."

Bonnie rolled her eyes.

Belle and I both laughed, and she whispered, "I'm pretty sure my daddy told me a similar story about his great uncle once, just a different town name."

"Me, too," I whispered back.

"Don't think I can't hear you," Henrietta said. "And your daddies, they were lying. Just copying our family tragedy is all."

Bonnie laughed so hard she set herself into a coughing fit. Henrietta slapped her on the back twice and nearly knocked her over. Once we all realized she wasn't in need of an ambulance, we laughed again. It definitely lightened the mood, and I was grateful. I'd all but forgotten that one of my friends could have been a double-murderer.

Until I caught her sitting in her chair glaring at all of us, and then I remembered.

～

Dylan called just as we were cleaning up at the end of class. Caroline helped pick up the discarded paper plates and swept the scone crumbs from the table.

"Everything go okay?" he asked.

"Hey, Mom. Yes, class went great, but I'm cleaning up at the moment. Oh, Caroline's here. Would you like me to say hey for you?"

"Got it. Call me when you've got a minute."

"Okay, I will. I'm getting ready to head back to the office, but I've got to drop her off first, so I'll call you back in a bit, okay?"

Dylan understood. "Talk soon." He disconnected the call.

I drove the few miles out of the main area of town to the Abernathy farm, and Caroline and I talked the entire way.

"I just can't believe Heather's gone," she said.

"I know. I'm in shock. It's just unbelievable…" I shook my head. "And heartbreaking."

She'd been leaning back in the seat, but she sat up and stared out the window of my car. "Well, at least maybe now my life can get back to normal."

I glanced at her, not sure exactly what that meant. "What do you mean?"

She rubbed the back of her neck. "Nothing. Things have just been stressful, that's all."

I wasn't sure how Heather's death would alleviate her stress, but if I wanted to find out, I needed to tread carefully. If she did kill my friends, I didn't want to end up her next victim. "We've all been through a lot, that's for sure. Heather and I weren't that close these past few years, but you two were. I know if something were to happen to Belle, I'd be a wreck, so I can imagine how you're feeling."

She kept her body toward the car door and focused on the outside view as it zipped by. "We weren't as close as you might think."

Okay, Lily, I told myself. Be careful. This could go really well or sink quickly into murky water. Choose your words with care. "I'm sorry about that. I had no idea."

"No one did, really. I never led on. It didn't fit in with my plan."

"Your plan? I…I don't understand."

She snorted but it wasn't an accidental snort from laughing. It was a purposeful snort filled with disgust and disdain. "Of course, you don't. Why would you? I mean, it's not like we've really stayed friends since college. You and Belle dumped us right after graduation. It's like we all came back to Bramblett County and y'all just up and stuck your noses in the air. I don't know what happened, but until now, all that sister talk meant nothing to you.

"I've had no one to talk to about any of this. I mean, first I find out my husband probably did cheat on me with Savannah and then I discover he and Heather might have been sleeping together recently, but could I confide in my lifelong friends, my sorority sisters even?" She flipped around in the seat and crossed her arms over her chest. She didn't say anything. She just sat there, her eyes burrowing into me.

I gripped the steering wheel, but my hands, sweaty with fear, struggled to stay in place. She was right. Not one hundred percent right, but pretty darn close. "Caroline, you could have come to me, and to Belle, too. Just because we don't talk everyday doesn't mean we aren't your friends." Besides, I wanted to add, but I didn't, that it took two people to be friends, and Caroline hadn't made a whole lot of effort either.

She smirked, but her eyes stayed cold and flat. I'd never seen her so angry. "I doubt that. You're too busy being little Miss Realtor and following that ex-boyfriend of yours around like a lost puppy. You don't have time for anything else. Speaking of puppies, I feel sorry for that one you got. He deserves a family that will give him some attention."

I swallowed back the venom pooling inside my mouth. I could take some slamming, but she'd gone too far. "It takes two to maintain a relationship, and I don't recall you putting a whole lot of effort into it either."

"I guess I didn't see the point since you'd made your feelings clear years ago." She tugged on her purse strap and wrapped it around her fist.

"Well, I'm here now. So, why don't you tell me what's going on? What's this plan you're talking about?"

"It doesn't matter. What's done is done. Heather's dead, and I don't have to act like I care anymore. Now maybe William can focus on me again instead of sneaking around with her." She opened her mouth, pushed her tongue forward between her teeth and then pulled it back and breathed out. "Like that was even sneaking around anyway. Practically the whole town saw them together. Even you did. Don't think I didn't catch what you were trying to do at the sheriff's office before. I'm not stupid."

"I never said you were."

"So, why didn't you come to me then? Why didn't you tell me you saw them together? If you were my friend like you say you are, you should have done that."

"I didn't want to say anything unless I knew for sure. I've been trying to find out what's going on. I even confronted Heather, and she basically threatened me and said to mind my own business. That's why Belle got salty with William. You know how she gets."

Caroline's face softened. "So, you told Belle?"

I pulled into the private drive for her home on the farm and shut off my car. "She saw them together, too. We both had the same thought as you, and we wanted to know the truth." I didn't tell her our reason, though.

"Did you confront William? Did he tell you anything?"

"No, we didn't. We haven't had the opportunity."

She leaned back in the seat. Her body, tense and tight, loosened. "I don't know what to believe."

I leaned toward her, took her hand in mine. "Honey, I will tell you this. When he brought you into class today, you were a hot mess."

She raised her eyes to me and sighed. "I know. I'm sorry."

I shook my head. "No, that's okay. That's not what I'm trying to say. My point is, William was genuinely worried about you. It was obvious. The concern in his eyes. You know how his eyes get all crinkly when he gets stressed? You used to talk about that in college. Said it happened during finals all the time, right?"

She nodded.

"He had that. He didn't want to leave you, but I could tell he didn't have a choice. I know he loves you. I don't think he was cheating on you with Heather, honey."

"You don't?" She bit her lip.

"A cheater doesn't worry about the person he's cheating on, not like that. That man loves you like crazy."

She clutched her chest. "Oh heavens, what is wrong with me? He does love me, doesn't he? And you're right. I have been a hot mess. I don't know what's going on. My emotions have been all over the place lately." She flung her arms around me and cried. "And look at what I've done to you. I'm a horrible friend."

I cried, too. "It takes two to maintain a friendship, remember? I haven't been that great of a friend, but I promise I will be better."

We talked for a few more minutes, and as she walked to her front porch, I sat in my car, more confused than I was before. Caroline's emotions went from one extreme to the other in a matter of minutes. Was that the sign of a killer or just a lost and confused wife?

I needed a minute to collect my thoughts, or more to disengage from them and relax. Instead of driving back to town, I drove into the parking lot of Abernathy Farms.

Fall season was just weeks away, and the corn for the maze was already fully grown and waiting for the design to be plowed in. The main sign said the design plan would be revealed on October first and had a burnt orange and hunter green count down sign next to it. The sign brought me back to my childhood and the excitement I felt knowing I'd be traversing through that maze soon and wondering what the design would be.

I'd grown up finding my way through the various mazes at Abernathy farm every season, from the Georgia Falcons logo to the Atlanta Braves logo and their World Series win, to my favorite, the Atlanta Aquarium. The memories flooded my mind, and I let the tears flow with the sadness of knowing Savannah and Heather, no matter what their sins, would never experience those wonderful memories again.

A harsh, loud knock vibrating on my window brought me back to reality. "Hey. You okay?"

I jerked to attention. "Oh, William." I'd left my car running, so I rolled down the window. "Yes, I'm fine. Just reliving old memories."

He kind of shook and nodded his head at the same time. "Must be tough for you right now."

"Very."

"It's been hard on Caroline, too. That's why my mom gave her those pills. Help calm her nerves and all."

"Are they still Xanax?" I asked. When I realized that question might have come off leading, I covered my tracks. "I'm wondering if maybe I should talk to my doctor about anti-anxiety meds or something? This whole situation has really been hard on me."

"I'm not sure. I think she gave her something different this time. My mom has a pharmacy of stuff in her bathroom. It's sad. She had trouble sleeping, and she said she's got a few prescriptions for sleeping pills, but I'm not sure which one she gave Caroline."

He rubbed his chin. "I hope it's not what's causing her to act the way she's been. Let me ask my mom what it was. Now I'm curious."

I nodded. "What do you mean, about the way she's been acting?"

He tapped into his cell phone, and as he did, he talked. I was impressed. I certainly couldn't do both.

"I think so, but I'm not sure. I told her she should go to the doctor, but you can imagine how well that went. She's just so moody lately, and I can't do anything right."

I waited, hoping for the right moment to ask him about Heather and Savannah.

"Hey, listen, I owe you an apology for how I behaved the other day," he said.

I raised an eyebrow.

"You know, when you saw me with Heather." His phone buzzed and he checked it. "Oh, it's Ambien."

I thanked him and then said, "You were a real jerk, so I'll have to think about accepting your apology."

"Okay. I deserve that."

I didn't break eye contact, but didn't speak, either.

"It wasn't what you think, Lily. I promise."

"What do you think I think, William?"

He held his palms up. "Come on. We both know what you think."

"Well, Heather certainly didn't deny it, so are you going to?"

"What? Are you serious?"

"She didn't admit to it either, but she didn't really have to. The way she threatened me made it pretty obvious something was going on between the two of you."

He blinked. "What? Heather threatened you? I swear Lily, that wasn't because of me. There was nothing going on between us, I promise."

"I'm not the only one that's seen you together, William. Belle has, and according to Caroline, other people have, too."

"Did…did…when did she say that?"

"Just a little bit ago."

He twisted around and glanced at his house, and then turned back to me. "It's not what it looks like." He swiped his hand over the top of his head. "This is bad. Real bad."

"She also thinks you were with Savannah in college, and I have to admit, I think you might have been, too. I have it from a good source you were."

He spread his legs apart and crammed his hands in his pockets. "Let me guess, Austin Emmerson is your source. Am I right?"

I didn't deny it.

"He's telling you what he thinks happened, not the truth. Yes, Savannah wanted to get with me, but no, it never happened. She had some crazy idea that she loved me, thought she could convince me to dump Caroline for her and that we'd get married and move to Atlanta together. I told her it wasn't going to happen. I never planned to leave the farm, and I never wanted anyone but Caroline."

When I didn't say anything, he added, "Austin couldn't stand me. You know that. And the reason was because he knew he was second choice to me, so instead of making it about him, he had to make me the bad guy."

Austin had a big ego, and I could see him feeling that way. I'd also watched William with Caroline during college, and even during high school. He'd been enamored with her then, and just that morning, the love still showed in his eyes.

Either William was telling the truth, or he was an incredible liar. "I don't even care so much about what happened with Savannah, but if you weren't cheating on Caroline with Heather, why have you been spending so much time with her?"

"Our anniversary is coming up. I asked Heather to paint a portrait of me and Caroline for a present. It was supposed to be a surprise. I gave her my wedding album, and we went to the different places in town that had meaning for us. That's why everyone's seen us together."

I nodded. "First Baptist Church."

"Where we got married. And the bridge is where I proposed to her, remember?"

I did remember.

"And you caught us coming back from the old barn last time. That's where..." He smiled. "well, I won't tell you what happened there."

I laughed. "I think I probably heard that story."

"I was paying Heather a lot of money for that painting, too. Enough to buy herself one of those condos on the Redbecker property."

"Caroline mentioned that."

"I need to talk to her. This has got to be why she's been acting so crazy." He leaned on my car window frame. "Thanks for telling me. I appreciate it."

"William, I don't know if you're telling me the truth or not, but someone told me something recently, and I'd like to share it with you."

"Okay."

"Secrets are never really secret. Especially in a small town."

As he rushed through the parking lot toward the field to his house, I sat back in my seat, even more confused than before. Both of my possible suspects gave me reasons to remove them from my list, while at the same time hinted to reasons their spouse should stay on it, front and center.

CHAPTER 12

I decided to wait until I got back to the office to call Dylan. I knew he'd pitch a fit about my conversations with both Caroline and William, but they weren't my fault, and I needed to get my thoughts in order to prepare for our discussion. I did send him a text to let him know I was okay and that I'd call him in a bit.

When I got to the office, the front door and what windows could be opened were, and Belle had a scarf wrapped around her mouth and nose. The foul odor assaulted my nasal passages before I even made it inside.

I covered my mouth with my shirt. "What is that God awful stink?"

Belle tossed me a scarf from her desk. "The Bramblett County sewage system, and it stinks to high heaven."

"Yes, it does. What's going on?" I wrapped the scarf around my face, but that didn't stop me from gagging. "Goodness, this is horrible. It smells like—"

"Like the gates of Hades opened up and every demon used our office as their toilet?"

"I wasn't going to be that descriptive but sure."

"Trust me, I'm a lady. If I wasn't, my adjectives would have been a lot more colorful."

"Have you called anyone?"

"No, I didn't think it was bad enough. Yes, I've called the plumber, but I think he got here, took a whiff, and took off running." She wrapped her laptop cord into a ball and placed it into her bag.

Ellie Jean walked in. "Oh, Lord. That stench could drive a maggot off a gut wagon." She held her nose. "Smells like you ladies got yourselves a burst sewage pipe. Have you checked your toilet?"

I glanced at Belle.

Her eyes shifted between the bathroom and me. "You're crazy if you think I'm going in there."

"Seriously?" I marched toward the back of the office, the rancid funk growing stronger the closer I got to the bathroom. When I opened the door, I gagged, shut the door, and ran back to the front of the office. "Oh, dear God. We definitely need that plumber, fast."

Dylan and Matthew walked in just then. Dylan, waving his hand near his nose, and Matthew pinching his shut with his thumb and forefinger.

"Whoever did that needs to see a doctor," Matthew said.

Belle laughed. Ellie Jean rolled her eyes, and Dylan and I tried hard to not laugh.

"Ladies, you cannot work here," Ellie Jean said. "Get your things. You're coming back to the library. You can work in the conference room."

Belle grabbed her bag, tossed the strap over her shoulder and headed toward the door. "Thanks, Ellie Jean. You're the best."

Dylan smiled at me. "You're going too, I assume?"

I nodded. "Definitely. Just need to grab a few things." I pulled some files from my cabinet, grabbed a few notebooks, and stuffed it all into my bag. "Thank you, Ellie Jean, your timing is perfect."

"Oh, sweetie, I was just taking a break and thought I'd stop by to set that appointment to discuss putting my house on the market, but I can't let you work under these conditions."

Dylan tipped his hat to her. "That's awful kind of you, Ms. Pruitt."

"Oh, now Sheriff, you don't have to be so formal. You can call me Ellie Jean like these two."

"Yes, ma'am."

I laughed. "I'll be there in a bit. Can we talk when I get there? I don't want you standing around here any longer than you have to, but I'd like to wait for the plumber."

"That's fine, sweetie. I'm going to grab me some sweet tea at Millie's and head on back. You get there when you can, and I'll have the conference room all ready for you."

"Thank you."

Belle and Matthew headed out, to where I wasn't sure, but I told her I'd wait for the plumber since she'd already suffered through the stink long enough.

Dylan used Belle's scarf to cover his face. I mentioned how it was quite fashionable on him. The pinks blended well with the browns in his uniform.

"Thank you. Our security guys are delayed. They'll be here in a few hours. Sorry about that."

"No, it's okay. I wouldn't want them working here with this smell anyway. It might kill them."

"I should send them a text and tell them to bring their Hazmat suits just in case."

"You're funny."

"So, how'd it go with Caroline?"

I detailed our conversation, and he wasn't upset like I thought he'd be. In fact, he was proud of how I'd handled it. "I'm glad you two worked things out, but that doesn't mean you shouldn't still be cautious."

"I was honestly taken aback by the things she said at first. She's so bitter and so angry, and then the next minute she's crying and apologizing."

"Angry enough to murder two people?"

"I honestly don't know." My eyes watered but not because of the subject of our conversation, because of the smell. "One minute I think it's possible, but then I think no, it can't be. I mean, she's been taking Ambien so clearly she's not sleeping, and God only knows what that's doing to her."

"How do you know it's Ambien she's taking?"

"I saw William, too. He told me. I guess his mom has a huge prescription collection, and they've been giving Caroline stuff because she's been struggling lately. First it was Xanax, but she hasn't been sleeping, so they gave her Ambien."

"So, it's not Caroline's prescription?"

"Nope. Why?"

"Because the preliminary reports say Ambien was the drug found in Heather's stomach."

"Oh, no." I leaned back onto my desk. "But wait. If Caroline's taking her mother-in-law's prescription, then wouldn't that mean that she's getting it from—"

"William."

"Oh, thank God."

He raised his eyebrow. "Um?"

"That means Caroline didn't kill my friends." Then it hit me. "Or that she did."

"There you go."

"I'm so confused."

"I know it's confusing."

"It is, but there's more to it than that."

He pressed his lips together. "Care to share?"

I filled him in on my entire conversation with William and specifically, what I said about secrets in a small town.

"Lily, you can't be going around trying to get people to talk like that. The more involved you are, the more you're putting yourself at risk."

"These are my friends. I can't not be involved." I paused when a tall man in a gray uniform walked in carrying a tool box.

"Oh, I smell a sewage issue goin' on here. Where's the pot? I'll take me a look."

I pointed toward the back. "That way."

He dipped his head. "Thank you, ma'am." As he passed me, he handed me his card. "Names Bobby Graves. Taking over for the local plumber. Can't remember his name now, but uh, I'm here in his place. Why don't you go on and get yourself a coffee or something? From the smell a things 'round here, my guess is this is going to take a while." He nodded to Dylan. "Sheriff."

Dylan nodded back. "Mr. Graves."

I thanked him, gave him my card and asked him to call once he knew what needed to be done. I also gave him the number for our landlord whose office was next door.

"I'll assess the situation and get with you in a bit. Don't you worry yourself none. It'll be fine I'm sure," he said.

I hoped he was as sure as he sounded.

"Let me drive you to the library," Dylan said.

"I have my car. I can drive."

"I'd like to talk more about William."

The thing was, I didn't. I'd already told him the entire conversation, and I'd reached my done level. I needed to hit the gym—something I hadn't done in forever—and cycle out some of the stress building up inside me or it was going to explode. "I'm not even going to the library yet. I'm going to the gym first. I need to destress before I go crazy."

"Okay. Let me know when you're back at the library."

"Can't your deputy on my tail tell you?"

He glared at me. "Just send me a text or something, okay?"

I nodded as he climbed into his car.

~

An hour and a half later I still hadn't heard from the substitute plumber, so I left a message for the office landlord and headed over to the library. Ellie Jean had been worried, and I apologized for not letting her know I'd gone to exercise.

"Oh sweetie, I understand. You've been under so much stress lately. Look at you, you're a hot mess."

I thought I'd pulled myself together okay after the spin class, but apparently not.

"How about I get you set up in the conference room again, and then I'll just run over to Millie's right quick and get you a sweet tea and a scone or something to hold you over until supper."

I had to admit, being catered to was heavenly. "Thank you, Ellie Jean, that would be lovely."

"It's no problem at all."

"Hey, has Belle been here yet?"

Ellie Jean turned before leaving the conference room. "Oh yes. She and that deputy were here, but they left to run some errands, she said. Told me to tell you she'd be back in later in the afternoon and not to worry." She waved as she left.

"Thank you." I unpacked my bag and set myself up in the familiar room. I checked my emails and followed up on a few client issues, handled some housekeeping details and then sat there and replayed the last few days over and over in my head.

First Savannah then Heather, both with connections far and deep. Add myself and Belle as potential victims and I had no idea what to think, but take us out of the picture, and the story wasn't too detailed, the possible killers only a few.

I played the game. Why would someone want the four of us dead? And could Caroline be added as a fifth? What in our pasts could justify our deaths so many years later?

I couldn't think of anything, not one single thing. Sure, I wasn't perfect, far from it, actually, but I couldn't recall ever doing anything to intentionally hurt anyone, or ever being involved in anything that made me guilty by association. And Belle? No, she wasn't perfect either, but the same went for her. Both of us were raised by strong parents that lived life by a certain set of rules, and we'd lived by those rules, too. I couldn't say the same for certain about Heather, Savannah, or even Caroline, but that didn't mean they deserved to die.

Nobody deserved to be murdered.

I worried, for the most part, that my conversation with William put me at more risk than anything I might have done in my past. I'd told him I suspected him of sleeping with both Savannah and Heather, and even though he denied both, if they were true, he knew I suspected it. Then I had to make it worse for myself by telling him secrets got around in Bramblett County. So, basically, I threw myself under the bus. And Belle, too, since she also saw him with Heather.

I called Belle to let her know what I'd done, but her phone went straight to voicemail, so I sent her a text message, and she didn't respond. I called her again and left her a message. "Belle, call me as soon as you get this, please."

Ellie Jean came in with a to-go cup of sweet tea and a bag with a treat from Millie's. "Here you go sweetie. This ought to do you right until you can get home and get something in your stomach."

At first I just sipped the sweet tea, but I ended up guzzling half of it down. I hadn't realized how thirsty I was. "Thank you. I guess I needed this."

"Oh, sweetie, you definitely needed it. When you have a chance, I'd like to bring you by my place to show you what I've done to get it ready to list with you and Belle. I mentioned it to her, and she said she'd be able to come by after work today. Will that work for you? I can have my assistant close the library if necessary."

I had hoped to start working with new clients after everything settled down, but it appeared Ellie Jean wasn't interested in waiting, and I probably could use the distraction. "What time does it close? I'll probably only work until six, but I have to get Bo at doggy daycare." I yawned. "I could probably meet you at your place around sevenish?"

"That would be wonderful. The library closes at six tonight, so I'll run home and clean up a bit and meet you there."

"Okay."

"You know where I live, right?"

"I sure do."

"Well then, I best be getting some things done before I head out," she said.

I finished the scone and the last of the sweet tea a few minutes after Ellie Jean left. I leaned back in my chair and closed my eyes. The days since Savannah's murder had taken their toll. I was give slap out. Just completely exhausted, I needed to sleep like the dead.

I tried calling Belle one more time, but she still didn't answer. I yawned again. I really needed a cup of coffee. The sugar and caffeine in the tea weren't enough. I knew Ellie Jean had coffee somewhere in the library, so I headed out to the main area and bumped right into William. I hit him so hard, I nearly fell over.

"Hey, steady there, Lilybit." He held me up. "You okay?"

"Yes, I'm…I'm just really tired." I found my balance. "What're you doing here?"

He held a vanilla file folder up. "Making copies. Our printer is broken, and it just didn't feel right going to Savannah's parent's company, even though they don't own it anymore. So, I'm here, using the copier."

"For free?"

"No, we have an agreement with the board. You know my dad's on it, right?

I yawned again. What was wrong with me? "Yes, I think Ellie Jean mentioned that the other day."

"We can use the printers and computers here whenever we want. Computers are free, but we get a bill for the printing at the end of the month."

"Oh, got it." William's face blurred. I didn't feel well.

"Let's just hope the flyers are okay. The Armstrong's usually make them, but I did it myself this time." He pulled one out of the folder. "Can you let me know what you think?"

I glanced at the flyer, and even though I was exhausted, and the flyer seemed a little blurry, I recognized the font immediately. It was the one on the note left on Savannah's door. The same one Dylan said was used to type Hannah's fake suicide note, and the one on the note left at my house. "Did you say you made this? On your computer?"

"Yes, I made it, but not on my computer. I made it here, at the library. On the rental computers. Easier to print that way."

"May I have one?"

"Of the flyers? Sure." He handed me one.

"Thanks. Hey, I hate to rush off, but I need to go." I struggled to keep my balance.

He grabbed my arm. "You sure you're okay? Let me help you. Where you going?"

I didn't want his help. The flyer. The pills. It all made sense. He killed them. He killed Heather and Savannah. I yanked my arm from his grip. "No, I'm...I'm okay." I lost my balance and steadied myself against the front desk. "I...I'm fine." I found my way back to the conference room and called Dylan, but it went straight to voicemail.

The last thing I remember was whispering Dylan's name into my phone.

CHAPTER 13

J woke up in a cold, dark room, sitting in a chair with my legs and hands tied tightly behind my back. I wiggled both my feet and hands but neither budged.

"If you would have minded your own business, the two of you wouldn't be here right now. I never had a problem with you two, and I hate that I'm going to have to kill you."

"Ellie Jean? Where's William?"

"Oh, don't you go and worry about that boy. He'll be fine. The lump on his head'll hurt for a bit, but I'm sure his momma's got something in that cabinet of hers to fix him right up." She laughed. "You ought to be worried about you and your friend here though, not anyone else."

"Belle? Are you here?"

I'm here, Lily. I'm okay."

"Oh my gosh," I cried. "I was wrong, Belle. I'm so sorry."

"It's okay, Lily. This isn't your fault."

Ellie Jean laughed. "Oh, sweetie, it most certainly is. If she'd just kept her nose out of it all, neither of you would be in this predicament, and come to think of it, neither would I. But here we are, and now I have to clean up this mess."

I needed to hear it from her. "Did you kill them? Did you kill Savannah and Heather, Ellie Jean?"

"Bless your sweet little heart, of course I did. A momma's got to do what she can to protect her baby, and that's what I did."

"What? Why? I don't understand." If she planned to kill me, I planned to die knowing why.

"You know why, Lily. They bullied my daughter, and that Savannah stole the competition cheerleading spot from her, and then Heather took her boyfriend, that handsome young man, Austin Emmerson."

"Austin? Faith didn't even know him," Belle said.

"Oh, she sure did. She went to church camp with him in high school, and they dated that entire summer after your senior year. Until he broke up with her for that floozy, that is."

"I had no idea," I said.

"No, you wouldn't have, because Faith wasn't important to any of you. You didn't even notice her, did you? She always said you were nice to her, but I told her just because you didn't bully her didn't mean you were being nice. She needed to learn the difference."

"So, you killed Savannah and Heather because of cheer-leading and a guy?" Belle asked.

"A mother's love knows no limits." She sighed. "Well, at first I was just going to frame Heather for Savannah's murder, but I decided she played a big part in my daughter's misfortune, too, so I killed her." The matter-of-fact tone of her voice sent shivers up and down my spine.

"When I saw Savannah, and I heard how upset everyone was that she was back in town, and I saw Caroline pitch her fit at Millie's, and I saw Austin while on my nightly walk the night before your class started, I just knew I had to do something. I figured it was the perfect time. I called Faith and told her Savannah was back in town, and she filled me in on what had happened between you girls, so I made me the perfect little plan.

And that's exactly what it was, perfect." She laughed, a wicked, snicker-like sound.

"How did Faith know what happened at Georgia?"

"Honey, there are no secrets in Bramblett County."

I seriously hated that expression. "You don't need to keep Belle here, Ellie Jean. You can let her go. It's me that you want anyway. I'm the one that's been asking questions. I'm the one that's been trying to find out who killed Savannah and Heather."

"That's not true," Belle said. "I've been trying, too. Don't let her fool you, Ellie Jean. I'm as responsible for this as Lily."

"Oh, heavens, look at you two, protecting each other like best girlfriends should. Why, if my Faith would have had a friend like that, we might not be in this mess now, would we?"

I stomped my feet on the ground, hoping the sound would help me guess where we were, but it didn't. I tried to focus, but my eyes just couldn't adjust to the dark. Ellie Jean had drugged me, and though the drugs had worn off some, I still felt them working through my system. My vision wasn't quite clear, and my head was surrounded by a thin fog.

I focused all of my energy on the area around me. I could see outlines of things, but nothing clear enough to determine anything familiar. Maybe shelving, but I wasn't sure. A stock room? I calmed my breathing and inhaled through my nose. Cleaning products. I smelled cleaning products. A storage closet maybe? In the library? "Where are we?" I yelled loud enough to see if my voice echoed, hoping to determine the size of the room.

Ellie Jean laughed.

I yelled again. "Where are we, Ellie Jean?" No echo. The room was small, so it had to be some kind of storage room.

"We're at the library, silly. What did you think I'd do, drag you out of here after drugging you? I'm getting on in years, I don't want to throw my back out. Lord knows it was hard enough having to take care of Savannah the way I did."

"Care to explain exactly what that was? If you're going to kill us, you could at least let us die knowing how this whole thing went down."

I heard the anger in Belle's voice, and I silently wished for her to calm down. The last thing we needed was for Ellie Jean to get angry and react.

"Oh, sweetie, it was like the Lord sent me a sign and told me what I needed to do."

"I don't think the Lord told you to murder two people," Belle said.

"You don't know how the Lord speaks to me."

"Belle, don't," I begged.

"When you girls had your first day of class, and Heather walked in with that red jacket, I remembered seeing Austin the night before in one just like that. I knew I'd have to get me one of those to make it look like Heather or Austin killed Savannah, but I didn't think one would drop in my lap the way it did.

When the girls started in on their cat fight, Heather took hers off and threw it over her chair. Do you remember that? You probably don't. You all were so busy trying to keep everyone calm." She laughed. "I was there, but no one paid me one bit of attention. I just walked over to Heather's seat and swiped that jacket right off the back of the chair and scooted right out of the conference room without anyone noticing. Later that afternoon I went to the craft store and picked me up a small tube of that red paint she couldn't stop talking about so I could put it all over the house. The sticky notes though, those were a bonus. I didn't realize you'd have those there, and they were the perfect place to add a little artistic touch, a way to frame the artist." She laughed again. "I'm proud of that."

"Definitely something to be proud of," Belle said, her tone one hundred percent sarcasm.

"That night I slipped on the hoodie, and I went to her house under the premise of asking for book donations for the library, and wouldn't you know it, she invited me in. Said she might could find a few to donate since it was her parent's house. She had the nerve to say she didn't believe in donating, that charity just encouraged people to be needy, but her parents wouldn't mind. That girl was so stuck up she'd drown in a rainstorm. I knew then she deserved what she had coming."

She took a breath and then continued. "So, when she went to look, I put it in the family room, and I just snuck up behind her, wrapped my hands around her neck and choked the life out of her. Didn't even know I had it in me. Dragging her lifeless body to the trunk was hard. Done wore me out. I stuffed her in there, put the red paint all over those notes you left, and then saw myself out.

"I realized I'd left my glasses there somewhere on my walk home, so I had to turn around and go back, and that's when I saw Austin Emmerson sneaking in through the back door. I waited for him to leave, hoping he didn't find my glasses, and scooted out the back door again."

She told her story like it made her happy, with no remorse, no regard for the life she'd taken. My hands trembled, and my pulse raced, but I kept my tone even and as casual as possible. I did not want to show fear. "So, you planned to frame Heather, but decided to kill her, too?"

"She deserved to die."

"Nobody deserves to die."

"A mother senses how her child feels, and I could sense Faith was happy. I knew just framing Heather wouldn't make Faith happy, but if Heather were to die too, that would, so, I killed her."

Acid climbed from my stomach and up my throat. I couldn't believe this sweet woman, my high school librarian, was a psychotic killer.

"Oh, and killing her was easy. I went to her house to tell her I'd spoken with the board, and they were thrilled to purchase three of her paintings and that I was approved to pick which three right then and there. She was thrilled because she wanted the extra money to buy furniture. Said she was buying herself a condo like me on the Redbecker property."

"As if you'll be doing that now," Belle said.

"Oh, honey, it's going to happen, you just watch." She laughed. "Oh, I guess you won't be able to, now, will you? Anyway, she invited me in, and we sat a spell, discussing the different paintings. She asked me what kind of budget I had. That's when I pulled out a letter I'd typed out from the board."

I laughed. "The font. She recognized it, didn't she? That's why she was on the floor, and the note was in the hallway."

"I knew that man of yours was telling you my business."

Belle snickered. "Your business? Woman, you haven't got the sense God gave a goose."

I grimaced. "Belle."

"Well, I just had to kill her then, for sure. I mean, I'd planned to and all, but not the way it happened. I'd taken the pills from Mrs. Abernathy's house already. That woman's had herself a drug addiction for years, so I decided to use those, but I knew they wouldn't work right away, so I had to smash them up right quick and put them in her tea. Then I strangled her like I did the other girl. But I didn't have a suicide note, so I had to rush back to the library and type one up right quick.

"I was back at the house and ready to set up her little suicide scene when you come knocking on her door. I didn't have time to get her on the bed, so I just left her there, lying on the floor. I waited for you to leave, and when you did, I tried to get everything set up again, but you came back with the sheriff, and I had to hide in her closet until I could finally make a run for it. The only reason I made it was because I threw that log at the side of his neighbor's house. I hoped that would give me some distance between us and it worked."

"You left the note for me, too, didn't you?" The question was rhetorical, but I asked anyway.

"I tried to warn you, but you didn't listen." She sighed.

"They're going to figure it out, Ellie Jean. They're already close to finding the owner of the font."

"To think, they had a suspect and would have brought him to trial, too, but nope. You screwed that up because of a stupid font," Belle said.

"But I killed her so she couldn't tell anyone."

"I recognized the font though, Ellie Jean," I said.

"And that's why I have to kill you now, too."

The room lit up like the Brave's stadium during a night game. The bright light hurt my eyes, but I didn't dare close them. Relief washed over me when I saw Belle staring at me from across the room.

Dylan walked through the door, his gun aimed straight at Ellie Jean. "I don't think that's going to happen. How about instead, you put your hands behind you? You're under arrest Ellie Jean Pruitt."

Matthew and two other deputies stood nearby, and I remembered there were two other deputies that had been watching me and Belle. I wondered what had happened to them.

Belle rocked her chair, and the legs bounced on the ground. "What took you guys so long? I've been here for hours, and I really have to use the ladies' room."

Matthew laughed, and the side of Dylan's mouth twitched. He gave one of the deputies a head nod, and the younger man rushed over to Ellie Jean and cuffed her wrists to the table. Another deputy untied me and Belle.

Belle made a beeline for the ladies' room. "Be right back."

I made a similar beeline, straight for Dylan's arms. "What time is it?"

"It's past midnight."

"Oh no, Bo."

"He's okay. One of the doggy daycare employees is at your house with him. I said you had an emergency."

I cried, a full throttle, ugly cry. Dylan hugged me, and I latched onto his body for dear life. "I thought I was going to die."

"I know, but you know I'd never let that happen."

Belle hugged Matthew, but she didn't cry. Once she let go of him, she charged toward Ellie Jean. "You listen here, you old woman—"

Matthew stopped her. "Belle, no." He pulled her back to him. "You don't want to do that."

Dylan read Ellie Jean her rights, and one of the deputies carried her off.

"Where is the deputy that was supposed to be watching me?" I asked.

"Whatever Ellie gave you that knocked you out, she gave to him, too. Put something in the tea from Millie's."

"What about Belle's deputy? What happened to him?"

"Food poisoning." He rubbed his chin. "Or at least that's what he thought. Now we're not so sure it wasn't just poisoning in general, seeing as the food came from Ellie Jean, too."

"She told us why she did it," I said.

"We'll need to get a statement, but first, I'm taking you to the hospital to get checked out."

"I'm okay. I don't need to go to the hospital. I just really want to see Bo."

"It won't take long at the hospital. A quick blood test and a checkup. I need to know what she gave you."

"I'm pretty sure it was Ambien. I drank that tea and about fell asleep right after. Ask William." I panicked. "Oh no. William, she's done something to him. We have to find him."

"We've got him. He's okay. He'll probably have a pretty bad headache for a few days but that's about it."

"I thought he did it. I saw his flyer and I tried to call you, but I…I don't remember what happened next."

"I do, and I'll fill you in later. Let's get you checked and then I promise, I'll bring you straight to the house so you can see your baby."

"Will you stay?"

He smiled. "I can't. I have to work, but I'll be back as soon as I can."

"Okay."

And that's exactly what he did.

~

I did finally sleep like the dead, and even though it passed in seconds, I needed those ten hours of rest like the desert needed rain. Dylan must have been worried, because the only reason I woke up was his repetitive pounding on my bedroom door.

"Why don't you just come in?" I finally hollered. "It's not like you haven't been in here a thousand times."

The door opened slowly. "I'm pretty sure you think I'm someone else."

I yelped and then yanked my pink and white duvet over my partially clothed body. "What? Oh, goodness. I thought you were Belle."

He leaned against my door frame, and the corner of his mouth twitched. "I bet you did."

Bo wiggled his tail and made little whiny, happy sounds at Dylan.

Dylan smiled. "Hey buddy."

Bo's tailed wagged harder, his Boxer booty in full swing, too.

The duvet rested under my chin. I pulled my arm out from under it and waved my hand toward the door. "Can you just give me a moment, please?"

He turned toward the hallway. "I'll be making coffee in the kitchen. With Bo. Go ahead and put on your flannels and a t-shirt." He winked.

I blushed. Bo jumped off the bed and followed him. The traitor.

Dylan closed the door, and I waited a few seconds before jumping out of bed and sprinting to the bathroom to rinse my face and brush my teeth. I threw on a pair of sweats, a tank top and an oversized sweatshirt—a red one with a hoodie—and when the smell of fresh brewing coffee hit me, I followed it to my kitchen.

"I really needed that sleep."

"I bet." He handed me a cup of java. "We released Austin. Ellie Jean confessed to everything."

"Good."

"What's wrong?"

"I actually thought Caroline or William could have been the killer." I set the coffee cup down on my kitchen table. "I feel horrible for that."

"Lily, we get this stuff wrong a lot of the time. You can't expect to get it right, either." He picked up my cup. "Come, let's sit outside."

We went onto my back patio. Bo followed. Dylan threw his tennis ball and Bo galloped after it only to be distracted by a dragon fly which he chased around the back yard for a solid fifteen minutes.

"It's natural to suspect people when lives tangle together like all of yours," Dylan said.

"I know, but I feel bad, and Caroline is so unbalanced right now. She's really upset about our friendship, too."

"You can still fix that."

"I know, and I intend to. There's a lot of things in my life I have to fix, and a few things I need to attend to, like the stink issue at the office."

"Yes, I know what happened there, too."

"You do? Did you talk to that Bobby guy? What was his last name?"

"I don't remember, but no, I didn't talk to him. Ellie Jean told me."

"How would Ellie Jean—oh, wait, don't tell me." I shook my hands toward him. "Hold on, how could she make the—"

He stopped me with a smirk. "She's a librarian with a specialized degree in research. With that kind of training and the Internet, she's got the world's how-to book right at her fingertips."

I crinkled my nose. "Ew. I hadn't considered that."

"I didn't think you would. Your mind isn't capable of thinking like that."

"Like what?"

"Like a murderer."

"No, I don't believe that it is."

"I'd appreciate it if you would set up the new password on the digital lock on your office door today."

"Is that how she got in?"

He nodded. "Said she'd been there bright and early that morning and laughed when she came by to check it out saw you and Belle and had the scarves wrapped around your faces."

"She has an ugly soul."

"Most killers do."

Bo gave up on catching the dragon fly when he discovered a toad in the grass. The toad hopped, and Bo jumped back, scared of the little brownish green monster barely a quarter of the size of his paw. It wasn't the first toad to scare him, and it wouldn't be the last.

"Bo, it won't hurt you unless you lick it," I said.

"I thought it would turn into a prince?"

"That's frogs, and I'm pretty sure that only happens in fairytales."

"Would you like to try it and find out?"

"What do you mean?"

He leaned in close and whispered, "Ribbit."

I laughed. "Bless your heart. You'll try anything, won't you?"

"To prove to you I'm here to stay? Yes."

My heart swelled. "I need to see Caroline."

He stood. "Okay, but I'm coming back tonight. I'll make you dinner."

I couldn't refuse.

 y first stop was Henrietta's place. Thankfully, I had her address in our class registration informa- tion. I'd called her on my way and asked if she could invite Bonnie over because I had something to give them both.

I didn't even have a chance to knock on the door before it swung open and the two older ladies smothered me with a dual bear hug.

"Oh, sweetie, are you all right?"

"Heavens, we were worried to death about you. How's Belle?"

"That Ellie Jean is a good for nothing snake," Henrietta said. They'd clasped their hands into mine and escorted me into Henrietta's home.

Henrietta shoved me toward her pink and gray early nineties couch. "Here, sit. I'm going to fetch you a glass of iced tea."

"Don't put any illegal prescriptions in it," Bonnie said.

"I don't have any of those," Henrietta shouted from the kitchen. "All of my drugs are legal."

I laughed. I hoped Belle and I could be carbon copies of Henrietta and Bonnie when we hit their age. Their zest for life was admirable and charming.

They squished on both sides of me and wanted all the dirt, so I gave it to them, everything, down to the most intimate detail, including the fact that at one point my fear level hit such an extreme I nearly wet myself. It surprised me, how cleansing and relieving it felt to release it all to them. They didn't judge, at least not me anyway. They had a massive vocabulary filled with choice words for Ellie Jean, and I couldn't disagree with any of them, but I kept my opinions about her to myself. Even though she wanted to kill me, a part of me understood her motivation. Her daughter had been wronged by Savannah and Heather, and yes, I was guilty by association in her twisted mind, so whether justified or not, she had a need to defend, to seek justice. I didn't agree with her decision or her actions, but I knew the love a mother felt for her child saw no boundaries and lived guided by no laws.

My mother always defended me, unless of course, I was wrong, then she'd make me own my wrong and make it right. But, if someone wronged me, they had better run. She would sic her sweet southern lady on the wrong-doer in such a way that would send them flying into the gates of Hades begging to be let in, just to sit a spell and rest. So, yes, I understood Ellie Jean's motivation.

"Okay ladies, enough about me. I have something for you."

Bonnie's eyes lit up. "A present?"

"Oh, sweetie, you shouldn't have. What is it?" Henrietta asked.

I retrieved two envelopes from my bag and handed them to the ladies. "Refunds for the class."

They both pushed their heads back and shook them.

"Oh, no, no, no." Bonnie said.

Henrietta pointed at her friend. "Yes, what she said. We don't want those."

I extended my hands and the envelopes out further. "Please, you deserve these. We haven't even finished the class and it just didn't go as planned. We can't take your money. Belle and I agreed."

"It may have not gone as planned—" Bonnie said, and then Henrietta continued for her.

"But it was a darn-tootin' blast."

"It sure was. We haven't had that much fun since the county fair in '69."

Henrietta made an O shape with her mouth, covered it with her fingertips and giggled. "Bonnie, you hush. We swore never to speak of that again."

"Oh, now don't get your undies all twisted in a knot. I'm not telling our secrets. I'm just saying it was fun, that's all."

I smirked. "You two know that secrets aren't ever really secret in a small town."

The two women covered their mouths and giggled.

"This one is," Bonnie said.

"And it's safe with us," Henrietta said.

"Well, I'll do my best to keep it that way, but only if you take these checks and promise to stay in touch." I put a check on each of their laps. "Otherwise, I might have to have a little talk with Old Man Goodson and Billy Ray."

"Oh, dear," Henrietta said.

"Well now, we can't have that, can we?" Bonnie asked.

Henrietta shook her head and plucked the envelope from her lap and stuffed it inside her dress and into her bra. "There, I took it."

Bonnie followed suit.

"So, how are your boys?" I asked.

"Oh, darling, they are working hard to keep up with us," Henrietta said.

"Darn tootin'," Bonnie said.

∾

My next stop was Caroline's, but even though we'd ended our last conversation on good terms, I felt I needed some kind of peace offering for thinking she could be a murderer, so I stopped at Millie's for a half dozen of her chocolate scones. Actually, I wanted seven, so I could munch on one while I drove.

Austin Emmerson sat at a table outside the café. I stepped back when I saw him, surprised he had been released already.

"They dropped the charges and released me late last night, or early this morning, I guess," he said.

"I'm glad." I pointed to the entrance to Millie's. "I'll be just a minute. Can you stay?"

He nodded. "I've got all the time in the world."

I placed my order with Millie and let her shower her love on me while I enjoyed every moment of it. She wanted the dirty details—her words—of my traumatic experience—again, her words, but I told her I just couldn't go into them and that I wanted, no, that I needed some time to heal before I talked about them. She understood. I asked if she'd bring my things outside, and she agreed.

I sat with Austin. At first, we just stared at each other, and then we both sighed. It was one of those, holy-cow, I can't believe that all happened kind of sighs from both of us.

He leaned toward me. "Thank you, Lily."

"For what?"

"For believing me. You were the only one."

"I…I uh…you're welcome." I rubbed my neck. "I did believe you, for the most part, but there were moments I wasn't sure."

"Of course, and I understand that. I wouldn't have known for sure, either, but even my parents thought I killed my wife."

"They did? That must be horrible knowing that."

He nodded. "My life will never be the same."

"I don't think mine will be, either."

He shook his head. "That woman. I can't...I can't believe she did this. All because of Faith Pruitt. And the thing is, I didn't actually date that girl. We talked a little at camp, and then she texted me afterwards, but that was it. We didn't have a relationship, so I don't know why she thinks we did."

"How did you find out about this?"

"One of the deputies told me. The one Belle's dating? Matt something or other."

I nodded.

"He told me the whole story. Wanted to know what was true and what wasn't." He leaned back in his seat. "And I'll confirm to you, the dating thing definitely wasn't."

"So, what happens now for you?"

"I don't know. Savannah's parents won't talk to me, and yeah, my parents were helping me with this, but you know, I just don't think I want to go back to my life. I don't know. I'm not sure what I'm going to do. I guess I need a little time."

"I can understand that."

"Are you okay? You know, really? That must have been scary."

I didn't want to say how I really felt. I just wasn't ready to deal with it. "Yes, I'm fine. I'm a lot tougher than I look."

He smiled. "You definitely are a tough lady. Dylan's one lucky guy, that's for sure."

I hoped it didn't show, but on the inside, not one part of me felt tough. The inside felt like a fragile glass vase ready to crumble into tiny pieces if just touched with a fingertip.

Millie brought out the scones, and Austin and I hugged goodbye. He promised to keep in touch, but we both knew that wasn't likely, and I was okay with that. I didn't mention anything about Savannah and William. I didn't see the point of bringing up the past again. It was time to move on, for everyone.

I took the scenic route to Caroline's hoping to practice what I wanted to say. Even though I went five miles under the speed limit, the drive wasn't long enough to decide on the right choice of words. It didn't matter anyway. I knew once I saw her, I'd have to wing it.

William answered the door. "You okay? We heard what happened. I feel responsible."

"I'm good." I searched his head for a lump or bump. "How are you?"

He showed me the lump on the back of his head. "The woman's pretty strong for her age. Dylan told me she said she smacked me with an encyclopedia. I'd left the library, but I just didn't feel right about leaving you there. You seemed...I don't know, stoned or something, and I felt bad leaving you like that. So, I went back in and the next thing I knew, Billy Ray was offering me a cup of sweet tea and a Band-Aid."

I laughed. "That's Billy Ray for you. Listen, I owe you an apology. I actually thought—"

He cut me off. I know. It's okay. We're good."

"You sure?"

He nodded. "I would have thought the same thing." He flicked his head toward the family room. "She's in there. She's got some exciting news for you, too."

I raised an eyebrow, but William didn't say anything more, he just led me to the family room.

Caroline was sprawled out on the couch with a glass of Coke® and a bag of boiled peanuts. When she saw me, she set the glass on the table and jumped up, sending the peanuts flying into the air. "Oh, for heaven's sake. Look at what I did."

I laughed. "You never were the cleanest girl in the house, were you?"

She stared at me, and we were both silent for a moment, and then we rushed to each other, crying.

"I'm so sorry, Lily. I know I already apologized, but I was just so ugly, and you didn't deserve that. I did not mean any of what I said. My hormones have just been a mess, and I didn't know what came over me, but now I do, and it all makes sense." She let go and smiled. "I'm having a baby."

My eyes nearly popped out of my head. "You're—a baby? Oh, Caroline, that's fantastic!"

She jumped up and down and hugged me again. "Oh honey, it's just the most amazing thing, isn't it? William is over the moon, he's so excited."

"So, you and William? You're okay?"

William interrupted. "We're better than okay." He smiled. "Here, let me show you something." I followed them into the den. Sitting on the couch were two large canvas paintings. One wasn't finished, but the other was. Both were of William and Caroline— one on their wedding day at the church, and the other the day they got engaged, at the bridge, and both with Heather's signature in the bottom right corner.

"William was the client Heather told me about," Caroline said. "The one that was paying her the big bucks for the paintings." She held up the finished painting, the one of the bridge. "This is my favorite. Not because it's finished, but because it's where I knew our lives were changed forever, right William?"

He smiled. "It's where she knew I truly loved her."

"He's right. I knew." She handed him the painting and rubbed her belly. "And now with this little one on the way, we've got even more love to share, and more changes to come."

"You sure do," I said.

"And this time, Lilybit, I want you to be more involved. No matter how busy you are, I'm going to need my girlfriends around. You hear me?"

I heard her loud and clear, and I planned to be there every step of the way. "Yes, ma'am."

"And I promise I will be just as involved as you because it takes two to make a friendship work. Someone very smart told me that."

We spent two hours talking about Heather and how we

planned to memorialize her. Savannah did come up, and I felt it was best to just leave well enough alone.

"I need to tell you something, Caroline." I wanted to apologize for thinking she could have murdered our friends.

She waved her hand, formed it into a fist and then pressed it to her mouth. "None of that matters now. It's time to move on." She rubbed her belly again. "We have a future to plan."

I realized in that moment she was right. The past didn't matter. I had a future to plan, too, and I intended to move toward that future that night at dinner.

I had two hours to prepare. Time was tight, but I could make it happen. I dropped Bo off with Belle for the evening, hit the grocery store and headed home. I set the table on my patio, hung my new string lights over the pergola, prepared Dylan's favorite appetizers; buffalo chicken dip—not at all romantic, but still yummy, and chips and salsa—and hopped into the shower. I left my hair curly, applied just a smidgen of makeup, and stepped into my blue and white floral sundress, the one he'd whistled at when he saw me in it the first time. I even put on a pair of heels. It was a big night, and I needed my big guns to hit the target.

When he knocked on my front door, I hollered that it was open and to come on in. I wasn't in the kitchen, though. I'd been in the family room, waiting.

"Lily? It's me. You shouldn't let anyone in without knowing who it is. You never—" He walked into the family room and stopped talking when he saw me standing there. "Oh."

I smiled. "Hey."

"Hey."

Everything I'd planned to say, everything I'd planned to do, I'd completely forgotten. It all left my brain the minute he walked into the room. His smile, his sparkling eyes, his sexy little slanted stance, it all erased my plan and instead, words rushed out of me like I was some blubbering idiot. "I'm sorry. I've been such a jerk. You haven't done a thing wrong."

His eyes softened, and the sides of his mouth curled into the sweetest smile I'd ever seen. I dug my feet into the floor to stop myself from climbing over the table to hug him. It didn't matter though, because he came to me and wrapped me in his arms.

"I'm sorry, too. I don't want you to feel like you can't trust me to be here, to love you."

"I can. I do. It's not you, it's me."

He laughed and then pushed me away. "That's a classic break up line. Are you sure you're not still breaking up with me?"

"I thought I already did that the other day?"

"Ouch."

"So, I guess we're even now?"

"If you're trying to apologize, you're not doing a very good job." He winked.

I pressed my lips together. "Oh, whoops."

"Like I told you before, I'm not leaving Bramblett County, Lily. I'm not leaving you. This is my home. You're my home. I came back here to be with you."

I backed away and walked to the other side of the couch. "I don't know, Dylan. I mean, I'm not sure you're the one for me."

His mouth dropped open. "What? How can you say that?"

I tapped my finger on my chin. "I just…I'm not sure. I need someone special. You know, a knight in shining armor, and I'm just not sure it's you." I tried hard not to smile, but the sides of my mouth edged upward anyway.

Dylan crept closer. "I think I might know a way to find out."

"You do?"

"I do." His face nearly touched mine.

"Care to share?"

He smiled and whispered, "Ribbit."

SIGNED, SEALED AND DEAD:
Lily Sprayberry Realtor Cozy Mystery #3

Small town folk don't always take care of their own.

As Bramblett County, Georgia realtor Lily Sprayberry preps for the annual community yard sale fundraiser, she discovers the body of the newly hired lacrosse coach lying in the high school gym.

At first, all signs point to natural causes, but when Lily finds an empty syringe lying under the bleachers, the coroner decides the coach was murdered.

Lily learns that the coach wasn't liked by the lacrosse parents, and when word gets out about his murder, the state athletic association suspends the program entirely.

A few of the lacrosse moms decide to take matters into their own hands, threatening someone close to Lily—her county sheriff boyfriend and his reelection status–by bullying Lily.

Soon, Lily's had enough. As she searches for answers, she's dragged deeper into an angry mob of high school sports parents all seeking revenge and gunning for their kids to sign with the most elite schools offering the best scholarships.

And some of them are willing to do whatever it takes, including murder.

When the killer figures out Lily is close to cracking the case, things take a dangerous turn, and Lily's life is on the line. Can she save herself, or will she be the next victim in Bramblett County?

**Get your copy today at
CarolynRidderAspenson.com**

KEEP IN TOUCH WITH CAROLYN

Never miss a new release! Sign up to receive exclusive updates from Carolyn.

Join today at CarolynRidderAspenson.com

As a thank you for signing up, you'll receive a free novella!

YOU MIGHT ALSO ENJOY...

The Lily Sprayberry Realtor Cozy Mystery Series
Deal Gone Dead
Decluttered and Dead
Signed, Sealed and Dead
Bidding War Break-In
Open House Heist
Realtor Rub Out
Foreclosure Fatality

Lily Sprayberry Novellas
The Scarecrow Snuff Out
The Claus Killing
Santa's Little Thief

The Chantilly Adair Paranormal Cozy Mystery Series
Get Up and Ghost
Ghosts Are People Too
Praying For Peace
Ghost From the Grave
Haunting Hooligans: A Chantilly Adair Novella

The Pooch Party Cozy Mystery Series
Pooches, Pumpkins, and Poison
Hounds, Harvest, and Homicide
Dogs, Dinners, and Death

The Holiday Hills Witch Cozy Mystery Series

There's a New Witch in Town

Witch This Way

The Angela Panther Mystery Series

Unfinished Business

Unbreakable Bonds

Uncharted Territory

Unexpected Outcomes

Unbinding Love

The Christmas Elf

The Ghosts

Undetermined Events

The Event

The Favor

Other Books

Mourning Crisis (The Funeral Fakers Series)

Join Carolyn's Newsletter List at

CarolynRidderAspenson.com

You'll receive a free novella as a thank you!